THE LAST WORD

ETTIE SMITH AMISH MYSTERIES BOOK 14

SAMANTHA PRICE

Copyright © 2017 by Samantha Price

All rights reserved.

No part of this book may be reproduced in any form or by any electronic or mechanical means, including information storage and retrieval systems, without written permission from the author, except for the use of brief quotations in a book review.

This is a work of fiction. Any names or characters, businesses or places, events or incidents, are fictitious. Any resemblance to actual persons, living or dead, or actual events is purely coincidental.

CHAPTER 1

While Ettie Smith was making dinner, she looked over at her older sister, Elsa-May, who was sitting quietly at the kitchen table. It wasn't like her sister to keep silent for any length of time and Ettie wondered what was wrong.

Elsa-May finally broke the silence. "How do you spell hello?"

The question struck Ettie as odd. Elsa-May was a very good speller, much better than she was. "How do you spell hello?"

"Jah."

"H-E-L-L-O." Ettie's voice was already strained from having to yell everything out to her sister over the last few days. Elsa-May's hearing was going downhill fast. Besides a sore voice, Ettie had a headache and felt like she was getting the flu.

"What?" Elsa-May shrieked.

Ettie put down the saucepan and walked closer. She tried her best not to sound impatient. "H-E-L-L-O."

"H-U?"

"*Nee!* H-E-L-L-O."

"*Denke.* There's no need to yell."

"Apparently there is," Ettie muttered looking over her sister's shoulder. "What are you doing?"

When Elsa-May looked up at her, her blue eyes fixed on hers and she must've taken a guess at what Ettie said. "It's one of Titus's crosswords. He gave it to me when we were at the meeting."

"I thought you said he was giving us a few next time."

"He only gave me the one."

"I hope he'll give you more than one next time. I'd like to have a go too."

"*Nee denke,* I'll wait until after dinner."

Ettie shook her head. "I said, I thought he was going to give you a few."

Elsa-May looked up at her. "What?"

"Never mind. You need to see about that hearing aid. Your hearing's not getting any better."

Elsa-May tapped a finger against her head. "You're losing your mind, Ettie. We didn't get any letters today. I already told you that."

Ettie sighed. Maybe she *was* losing her mind, but it had nothing to do with any letters. She'd make an appointment tomorrow and take Elsa-May back to the doctor before she drove her completely mad. For now, she continued making the dinner.

Elsa-May said, "It wonders me how he makes these crosswords. It's got to be difficult."

"I wouldn't be able to do it. It keeps his mind active."

Elsa-May turned back to her crossword. "What is a lyric, or poem of some length?"

"Is it an ode?" Ettie suggested.

"I didn't say a bad smell, I said—"

"I know what you said, and I said, is it an ode—not an odor."

"Oh, an ode?"

"Jah." Ettie's patience was wearing thin, but she reminded herself her sister couldn't help mishearing everything.

Elsa-May looked back at the crossword. "O-D-E. That fits. *Denke,* Ettie."

Ettie sighed. And then thought about Titus and his crosswords. He'd been doing them for years. Exactly how did he create them? Did he start with the words first or the clues? Ettie chuckled to herself. He would've had to start with the words, but he had to be clever to have the words intersect like they did and fit into that little square box. No doubt the crosswords in the newspapers were generated by computers. Nowadays computers did everything.

Ettie wrote down a message on a piece of paper and handed it to Elsa-May, rather than shout at her and make her throat sore. The message said that first thing in the morning, she was going to call Elsa-May's doctor and have him refer her to a hearing specialist.

Elsa-May read the note and looked up at Ettie. "I can make that call myself."

Ettie pressed her lips together and wrote again on another bit of paper telling Elsa-May that she might not be able to hear what the person on the other end of the line said. Elsa-May read it and then reluctantly nodded in agreement for Ettie to make the call.

THE VERY NEXT day after they had finished an early breakfast, Elsa-May said, "Why don't you take Snowy with you when you call the doctor?"

Ettie nodded and clipped the leash onto his collar. "Come on, boy," Ettie whispered. "Let's you and I get out of this mad *haus.*"

"What do you mean, *mad haus?*"

"Nothing," Ettie said, hurrying toward the door.

How could her sister hear her low voice when she could barely hear her when she yelled?

"Try and make the appointment for today if you possibly can. Tell him your mad *schweschder* is making you mad, so it's urgent."

"Oh, I will," Ettie said before she closed the door. "Before I lose my voice completely."

Ettie and Snowy walked to the end of the road to the shanty where the telephone was housed. She carefully leaned down and tied Snowy's leash onto a nearby pole. Then she pulled the doctor's card out of her sleeve and dialed the number. After she told the receptionist who and what the appointment was for, she held her breath hoping to get her in to see the doctor that very day.

"We have a cancellation at two thirty. Would you be able to bring your sister in then?"

Ettie quietly thanked God. "Yes, we'll take that appointment." Delighted, she made her way back home to tell Elsa-May the good news. When she was halfway home, she realized she'd left Snowy tied up back at the phone. She turned around to see Snowy staring after her and looking most upset.

"I'm coming, Snowy," she called out. Elsa-May would've been horrified if she had gone home without him. She untied his dog's leash and they made their way back home.

Instead of telling Elsa-May two, or possibly three times, she let Snowy off the leash and then wrote down the appointment time and showed her.

Elsa-May looked up at her. "Today?"

Ettie nodded, and then used her loudest voice. *"Jah,* today. You might have to get a hearing aid. I've heard they're quite expensive."

"Don't worry about me. I don't get nervous going to the doctor."

Ettie got closer and spoke slowly. "I said hearing aids might be expensive. Cost a lot of money."

Elsa-May's lips turned down at the corners. "I won't get one if they cost too much. I'll just get one of those shoe horns."

"A shoe horn?" Ettie yelled, confused.

"Jah."

"A shoe horn is for helping put your shoes on." Elsa-May laughed and then Ettie realized what she meant. "You mean one of those old-fashioned horns they used to use?"

Elsa-May nodded. *"Jah."*

They both laughed and Ettie was pleased that she hadn't had to repeat her last sentence.

Ettie waited patiently in the doctor's waiting room while Elsa-May saw the doctor. Hopefully, he was organizing a referral to a hearing specialist. The sooner she got hearing aids, the better. Ettie flipped through a few magazines to fill in time. After skimming through the fifth one, she realized someone had sat down next to her. She looked over and saw that it was Elsa-May. "That took ages. Did you get the referral?"

"I can hear."

"Nee, you can't!" Ettie was just about to march into the doctor's office and tell him so herself.

"Ettie, listen to me. I had severe wax build-up in my ears, and now I can hear perfectly well. The doctor just got rid of it all."

"Is that it?"

"I just said the build-up was quite severe, and it was in both ears. I didn't realize there was so much I couldn't hear until he cleared my ears."

"The wax must've been like solid rocks. So, you can hear me?"

Elsa-May smiled. "I can hear you perfectly well."

Ettie was astounded.

Just as they were walking outside, they ran into Maureen Palmer from their community.

Maureen was by the steps of the doctor's. "Hello, you two. Have you heard what happened?"

Elsa-May and Ettie looked at one another, and then Ettie said, *"Nee,* what?"

"Titus Graber is dead."

Ettie was surprised to hear of the death of a man so young. He would've only been in his mid-sixties.

Maureen looked from Ettie to Elsa-May and her eyes flickered with fear. "He was found murdered only just today in his home."

Elsa-May gasped. "Murdered?"

"That's dreadful," Ettie said. "Do they know who did it?"

"Nee. I don't think so. I don't know much about it. I can only tell you what I heard from someone else. I better go inside now, or I'll be late for my doctor appointment." Maureen pushed past them.

Ettie and Elsa-May went home in a taxi, trying to get over the shock of Titus being killed.

Elsa-May's bottom lip quivered. "I can't believe it. I was just doing one of his crosswords."

"I know. He kept to himself, but everybody liked him. He'll be missed."

Elsa-May shook her head. "And Maureen said he was killed in his home."

CHAPTER 2

They were only home in enough time to eat a quick sandwich as a mid-afternoon snack before there was a knock on their front door. Elsa-May got off her chair to answer it, and Ettie managed to grab Snowy's collar as he ran past her feet heading to the door. He always tried to jump up on visitors. Ettie figured it was someone else come to tell them the news about Titus.

Then she heard Elsa-May say, "Detective Kelly, come in."

Immediately Ettie picked up Snowy, and called out, "I'll put Snowy outside." She knew Snowy had a liking for the detective, but the feeling was not returned. Kelly had to be there regarding Titus.

When Ettie came back to see the detective

already sitting down and talking to her sister, she sat also.

"How do you know already?" he asked. "I've only just told his next of kin. How did you hear?"

"We've just come back from town and Maureen told us."

"Do I know her?" he asked.

"Nee, she's someone from our community," Ettie said.

"How did she—"

"We didn't ask," Elsa-May said, cutting him off.

Ettie asked, "How did he die?"

"Who do you think might have done this?" Kelly asked.

"No one in our community," Elsa-May said.

He shook his head. "That's what you always say."

"And we're always right."

The detective stared at the two of them.

"Would you care for a cup of hot tea?" Ettie asked.

He raised his eyebrows. "How about a coffee?"

"Certainly. I'll do it, Ettie." Elsa-May grabbed the sides of her chair and pushed herself to her feet.

Ettie stared at the detective. "Did you see any clues?"

"Clues?"

"Yes, something that might have told you who did it."

"I know what a clue is, Mrs. Smith." He shook his head. "I can't tell you too much at the moment."

"Who found him?"

"A man by the name of Max Burley."

"That name's familiar."

"He found a syringe sticking out of Mr. Graber's neck."

"Oh, that's horrible!"

"Yes, it is. We still don't know what type of poison killed him, but we will soon."

Elsa-May brought Kelly a cup of coffee, and placed it on the low table beside his chair. "There you go."

"Thank you."

"Did you hear that, Elsa-May?"

"What was that?"

"Detective Kelly just said that there was a syringe sticking out of his neck."

Elsa-May gasped and covered her mouth. "He was poisoned?"

"It looks that way. We'll know soon."

"Elsa-May, don't we have any of that fruit cake left?"

"No, don't trouble yourselves. I'm fine, thank you," Kelly said.

"I ate the last of the fruit cake, but we do have that lemon cake with the thick icing."

Kelly smiled. "Did you say lemon cake?"

"Yes, would you like to try some?" Elsa-May asked.

"I'd love to. Lemon cake's one of my favorites."

Elsa-May headed back to the kitchen and Ettie was pleased that Elsa-May's hearing loss had only been a short-term thing.

Kelly was being pleasant today, and that only meant one thing. In the recent past, Ettie had noticed that Kelly was only nice to them when he wanted something. He put his coffee on a nearby table and Elsa-May handed him a plate of cake along with a paper napkin and a cake fork.

"Thank you." He looked up at the two of them. "Aren't either of you having anything?"

"We've only just eaten."

His eyes gleamed when he stared down at the cake. He stuck his fork in, broke off a piece, and then popped the portion into his mouth. As he savored the burst of sweet citrus, he closed his eyes.

Ettie wondered how long it would take him to get around to asking them if they'd help him. She was certain it was the only reason he was there. Nearly every time there was a crime involving an Amish person, Kelly landed on their door, cap in hand, asking for help. This time, he was drawing things out. Ettie figured he was treading gently because he'd been impatient with them on their last few encounters.

Elsa-May licked her lips, Kelly's obvious enjoyment making her wish she'd gotten herself a piece of that cake. "Did you only stop by to tell us about Titus, or was there something else?"

He stared at her with cake crumbs sprinkled around his mouth. "I figured he was in your community and I thought you'd like to know. Anyway, a man's died, that's enough, isn't it?"

"More than enough, that's true, but I'm guessing you want our help with something?" Elsa-May stared at him.

He placed the plate down next to his coffee. "I had hoped you would've offered." He then stared at Ettie.

"Offered what?" she asked.

"You normally can't wait to find out what happened."

"Does that mean you want us to help you?" Ettie asked him.

He sighed. "If you wouldn't mind, I'd appreciate some help with this one."

"You're not losing your touch are you, Detective?" Elsa-May asked.

Whipping his head around to look at Elsa-May, he blurted, "No!"

"Why are you asking us for help this time?" asked Ettie. "It's only in the early days. I mean, you only found him today. There can't have been that many roadblocks."

"No, Mrs. Smith, but I just get an uncanny feeling about this one. And I knew you'd be interested since the deceased was Amish."

"Can we think about whether we'll help this time?"

Elsa-May added, "It's just that people in the community know that Ettie has helped the police out from time to time with talking to our members, and what not, and some folks aren't happy about it."

"No, they don't like it," Ettie said. "They don't approve."

"I know you Amish are peaceful, turn the other cheek and all that, but there's no time to think about it. If you're going to help me, you'll need to do it now." When they remained silent, he continued, "I thought you'd both want justice." He raised his hands. "Wait a minute. I'm not going to get caught up in that subject again. Please don't comment on what I just said. I don't need to talk about religion." He reached for his coffee and took a few sips. Then he set his cup back down on the side-table and lifted his plate of cake close. "Mrs. Smith, all I want you to do is tell me about the people surrounding the deceased and also tell me about what kind of man he was, and so forth."

"We can do that."

"Good." He dug his fork back into the cake. "Can you meet me first thing tomorrow at the station?" Before they could answer, he added, "Better still, I'll come here and collect you."

Ettie looked at Elsa-May and when she didn't give an expression of disapproval, Ettie thought it would be okay to agree with what the detective asked. "Okay. We'll be waiting. What time?"

"Is eight too early?"

"No."

"We'll be ready and waiting," Elsa-May said. "We're always up and about early."

"Good." He ate another mouthful. "Who made this cake? It's delicious."

"Elsa-May made it," Ettie replied, wondering if he was trying to butter them up. Then again, he did like cake.

Elsa-May said, "If he was found dead today, I hope the family has been told. There are his sons, Albie and Simon, and then—"

"That's all under control. I went to Simon's house and informed him and he gave me his brother's address, which I already had, and his mother's. Another officer informed Titus's ex-wife, Sophie."

"And you talked to Albie, the son who's still in the community?"

"Yes. You can tell me more about his family tomorrow."

Ettie looked at the way he was finishing the last mouthfuls of cake. "Are you in a hurry, Detective?"

"Yes, I'm trying to get home to my wife at a reasonable hour."

Ettie and Elsa-May looked at one another, brows raised in surprise.

"Wife?" Ettie asked.

"Yes." A smirk appeared around Kelly's face. He looked pleased with herself.

"This is the first time we're hearing about this."

"Since when have you been married?" Elsa-May asked.

Kelly chuckled. "I've only been married two weeks."

"Where did you meet her?" Ettie asked at the same time as Elsa-May said, "How long have you known her?"

"I turned down the wrong street and as I was about to do a U-turn and go back, I saw a woman standing by her car. She looked so helpless I knew that her car had broken down."

"It must've been a quick romance," Elsa-May said.

"It was."

"A whirlwind romance," Ettie added.

"You didn't mention her the last time we saw you."

"I hadn't met her then."

"We must've only seen you three months ago. Do you mean to tell me that you met, courted, and married the woman in a matter of weeks?"

"That's right. She's a unique woman, a little younger than me, and she's never been married. She's a career woman, so she understands the hours I work. And my lack of sleep. She's understanding."

"And are you hurrying home for dinner just now?"

"That's right."

"We won't keep you," Elsa-May said with a twinkle in her eye.

"Thanks for the coffee and cake." He rose to his feet.

Ettie pushed herself off the couch. "I just hope the cake didn't ruin your appetite."

"There's no chance of that. Although I have noticed my girth's increasing since I got married. My wife's a fine cook."

They walked the detective to the door. When he got in the car and drove away, they closed the door, and then the two sisters looked at each other and laughed.

"I can't imagine Detective Kelly married," Elsa-May said.

"And all the complaining he used to do about his life and never having time for a relationship. Now he's got one."

"He certainly must've found the time in the last few weeks."

"He must've. I wonder what she's like."

"She must be attractive enough to have caught his attention as she stood there hopeless and helpless by her car that day."

Ettie sighed. "It's funny how things happen sometimes. He took a wrong turn and just like that there she was."

"Most wrong turns take people to a bad place, but this wrong turn was the right turn, since it helped him to find a wife."

Ettie tapped her chin. "I wonder how much he knows about her."

"He's a detective, he must have checked her out thoroughly."

"Do you think so?"

"Of course he would've. He would've found out her name and run her through the system the first day he met her." Elsa-May sat in her chair and fished her knitting out of the bag by her feet.

"I suppose you're right," Ettie said.

"I usually am."

"Now, is there any of that lemon cake left? I could hardly stand watching Kelly eat his piece. He enjoyed it so much it made me hungry for some."

"There's only a slight amount left for me."

Ettie put her hands on her hips. "And what about that diet?"

Elsa-May chuckled. "We'll split it in half."

"That sounds more like it," Ettie headed to the kitchen to get them some cake.

"How about we keep that lemon cake company with a cup of hot tea?"

"Jah, Elsa-May, you just keep on knitting, and I'll do everything."

"Okay, and after that you can open the back door and let Snowy back in. Also, have you given any thought to the evening meal?"

"We're using up the leftovers." Ettie heaved a sigh. She opened the dog door and Elsa-May's fluffy white dog scampered inside. As usual, his first order of business was checking out every spot where he could catch a trace of Detective Kelly's scent.

By the time they had finished their lemon cake and tea, the sisters were thinking less about Kelly being married and more about Titus being murdered.

"I can't believe it, I just can't believe it," Elsa-May said.

"Neither can I, but it's happened."

"I can only imagine how awful his poor family feels."

"Did you finish the crossword?" Ettie asked.

"Not yet, but that'll be the last one he'll ever give me. I've only half finished it. There's always a couple of words I just can't get."

"Me too, that's why I lose interest after a while. I wonder... Why do you think Titus liked his crosswords so much?"

Elsa-May said, "Perhaps they're easier to construct than they are to figure out. Or maybe it was the challenge. He's a man who likes challenges, maybe."

"I think it would be quite hard to make a crossword. I was thinking about that earlier."

"Do you think Kelly seemed a bit softer today?" Elsa-May asked.

"I do, but I just thought he was being nice because he wanted us to do something. Then we find out he'd gotten married and hadn't even told us. He should've invited us to the wedding."

Elsa-May chuckled.

"You'll have to wake up early to take Snowy for a walk before we leave tomorrow morning," Ettie said.

"Nee, I'll do it in the afternoon."

"Elsa-May, you know if you don't do it first thing in the morning other things get in the way through the day."

"Okay, but I won't walk if it's too cold."

"It shouldn't be. The weather's been mild." When Elsa-May didn't say anything further, Ettie looked over at her. "Why are you looking into space like that?"

"I'm just wondering how long it will take the wax to build up again in my ears. It was kind of nice not being able to hear your nagging all the time."

"Nagging? You couldn't hear *anything* I said."

Elsa-May pressed her lips together. Then she put her knitting back into her bag. "I'm off to bed."

"I guess that leaves me to do the washing up?" Ettie stared at the teacups and the plates. They'd decided it was late enough by now that they didn't even need an evening meal.

"Denke, Ettie," Elsa-May pushed herself up from her chair and walked to her room. Snowy was not far behind her.

CHAPTER 3

The next morning, Ettie and Elsa-May didn't wake as early as they'd wanted. They were just finishing breakfast when Detective Kelly knocked on the door. When Snowy heard it, he raced to the front door and started pawing at it. Elsa-May scooped her dog into her arms and then opened the door.

Kelly smiled when he saw Snowy and reached out to pat his head.

"We'll be ready in one minute," Elsa-May said.

"Very good. I'll wait in the car."

Ettie wasn't far behind Elsa-May and didn't know whether she liked this mild-mannered dog-liking Detective Kelly. He seemed like a stranger.

The sisters quickly got organized and as they

drove away from the house, Kelly said, "I'm going to take you to Titus's house."

"That's quite a distance. He lives the furthest from the bishop's house out of anyone in the community," Ettie said. "And the furthest away from town."

"That's where we're going. The evidence technicians were there for some time, but they've been and gone."

"Why are we going there?" Elsa-May asked.

"It's somewhere to start, and we can have a chat there."

"You want us to tell you about Titus when we're at his house?" Ettie asked.

"Yes. Why not?"

"Okay. We don't mind," Ettie said. "I suppose."

After a twenty-minute journey, they traveled down a long driveway to get to Titus's house. Compared to the size of his land, his house was just a shack, but like all Amish people, Titus lived simply. Ettie had only been to his house once before when she was with a group of ladies organizing a fundraiser.

"Elsa-May, isn't the charity auction on tomorrow?"

"That's right it is."

"The one Titus was organizing?" Kelly asked.

"Yes, how do you know about it?" Ettie asked.

"There was a lot of paraphernalia around the house, paperwork and bits and bobs about the auction. What part did Titus play?"

"He always helped out charities by organizing stalls and getting people to donate goods to put up for auction."

"He sounds like he was a good man."

"Yes, he was. A very good one," Elsa-May said. "He'll be sorely missed."

Kelly looked out the car at the barren landscape. "What does he farm on all this land?"

"I'm not sure, but from the looks of the land he hasn't farmed it for some years. He could've been living off his savings. He would've made a bit of money over his time."

"And who do you think will reap the benefit of that now?" Kelly asked, still driving.

"Probably the son who stayed in the community."

"Ah, yes, Albert."

"Yes, but he's always gone by Albie."

"I'll be talking to all of his family again, and I'll talk with his close friends and whomever he worked with on these charities."

Kelly finally stopped the car just outside the house. The ladies stepped out of the car and walked toward the front door over small white crushed-rock pebbles that crunched underfoot. When she looked up to see where the pebbles started and finished, Ettie noticed that they appeared to run around the entire perimeter of the house.

They waited for Kelly to open the front door with the keys he was jiggling in his hand. Once he had unlocked it, he held the door open for them. "Go in, have a look around. Try not to touch anything."

Ettie said, "You said your people have finished in here."

"They have, and they've taken prints and photographs, but just do your best not to disrupt anything."

"You want us to take a look around?" Elsa-May asked Kelly.

"Yes."

Ettie went into the room off the end of the hallway, which was the kitchen. When she looked at the papers on the kitchen table, she saw some scribbles on a paper, something to do with his crosswords, along with a dictionary. "Come and look at this, Elsa-May. This is how he did his crosswords. He used a dictionary." Ettie pointed at pages of empty crossword grids that were tucked partly under the dictionary.

"Well, I suppose he would've used one."

"Isn't that cheating?"

THE LAST WORD

"Nee, it's not. He can't have known every single word and its meaning."

"I guess you're right."

"That's where he died. Right there." Kelly pointed to the kitchen table.

"What do you mean?" Ettie took a step backward.

"He was sitting in this chair slumped over one of his crossword puzzles."

"Oh, that's awful," Elsa-May said. "Where is that crossword now? The one he was working on"

Ettie asked before the detective answered Elsa-May's question, "Did you find out the cause of death yet?"

"We're still waiting on the toxicology reports to come back."

Elsa-May shook her head. "To think he was murdered in his own home."

"Doing one of his beloved crosswords," Ettie added.

Kelly waved a hand in the air. "As you can see, there was no sign of a struggle and there was no forced entry."

Elsa-May said, "That's because he probably didn't have his door locked. What was the point? He lived so far away from anyone. He should've been able to hear someone coming with all those pebbles around the house. I wonder if that was why he had them there."

"We rarely lock our door," Ettie said.

Kelly didn't breathe a word and Ettie turned her attention to some crosswords she saw on Titus's kitchen countertop. He had a list of words down one side of a piece of paper. Then on the other, he'd filled out a crossword grid with those words. He'd been writing a list of *down* and *across,* for the prompts for those words. "Is this all that was here?" Ettie asked Detective Kelly, lifting up the papers. "These are to do with his crossword puzzles."

Kelly stared at the pages. "Put them down, Ettie. There was more, but it was taken into evidence. This is right where he was found, right here." He took two steps to the right and tapped the table. "His head was resting on paper and the technicians took all the papers that were close to him."

Ettie nodded, a bit embarrassed that she forgot his request not to touch anything.

"Now you've got a sense of his world. Tell me all you know about Titus Graber."

Ettie looked at Elsa-May to see if she wanted to talk first.

"He was a kind man," Elsa-May said.

"Not kind enough for his wife to stay with him," Kelly said.

"People leave a relationship for many different reasons. We're not sure why his wife chose to leave him and the community. It might not have had much to do with Titus."

"When did she leave?" he asked.

"Hmm, it would be around ten years ago, wouldn't you say so, Elsa-May?"

"I thought it was more like fifteen."

"Either way it was a long time ago. The two boys were grown up at the time."

"Yes, they were," Elsa-May confirmed.

Kelly stood staring at the two of them with his arms folded. "You mean to tell me that the two of you have no idea why his wife left?"

Elsa-May answered, "I can't recall. If I knew once, then I've forgotten."

He shook his head and looked downward. "Amazing."

"Do you want us to find out?" Ettie asked.

"Not for the moment. There might be other things I want you to find out for me, though."

Ettie took a step closer to Kelly. "Who do you think did it?"

"We have to go through all the evidence before we can make any assumptions, but it's always the nearest and dearest who are of the most interest to us."

Ettie knew he wouldn't tell her anyway, even if he had a suspect right now, but from the way he was talking it seemed he suspected Titus's ex-wife, Sophie. "I imagine that even though Sophie wasn't divorced from Titus, that she would've been very upset."

"They weren't divorced?"

Ettie knew Kelly would've known they weren't. He would surely have checked and was trying to get more information from them. "No. They were separated and, as you know, she was out of the community." Could she have had no alibi for the time he was murdered and that's why he suspected her? "What time of day was he murdered?"

"It's been estimated the time of death was around ten o'clock at night, and he wasn't found until morning."

"Who found him, again?"

"A man by the name of Max Burley."

"Oh yes, that name sounded familiar when you told us yesterday, but I can't place him. He was an *Englischer?*" Ettie asked.

"Yes."

"Ettie, isn't he the man who has some involvement with the charity auction tomorrow?"

"That's right. *Jah,* I think so."

"You're correct about that. He told us he's the

founder of the charity and that Graber gave him a lot of help with fundraising."

Ettie knew Kelly wasn't being open with them. They'd mentioned the charity before and Kelly hadn't told them that the man who discovered Titus's body was the founder of the charity. Kelly was up to something. Unless this was the new Kelly, the new 'married' Kelly.

"Is there anything else either of you can tell me about his family?" Kelly asked.

"Albie bought himself a house and moved out, Simon left the community and then Titus's wife left."

"And how did husband and wife appear to get along when they were living together?"

"Just normal," Elsa-May said.

"There was never any talk that there were problems within the marriage," Ettie said.

"Interesting, and are both of you going to the charity auction tomorrow?"

Ettie shook her head. "No, we don't go to those things anymore."

"They're a bit too tiring. They go on all day."

"Surely you could go for only part of the day," he said.

Ettie narrowed her eyes at him. "You want us to go?"

He nodded.

"You think the charity auction had something to do with his death?" Elsa-May asked.

"I don't know at this stage, but I'm keeping an open mind. I'll stop by the auction tomorrow myself. I was hoping you two would also go to keep an ear to the ground and see what you might find out for me."

"You could find out all you need to know from Max, couldn't you?" Ettie asked.

"It's not the workings of the charity I want to find out about."

"Of course not," Elsa-May said.

"We could go for part of the day like the detective said, Elsa-May."

"Okay, why don't we do that?"

Kelly nodded slowly. "Good, thank you. I would appreciate it."

"Ettie can do what she does best, and that's talk to people."

"Yes, that's the plan," he said.

Ettie looked down at the gray linoleum flooring. It had been swept clean. It certainly hadn't been that clean last time they were at Titus's house.

Detective Kelly looked around. "It's rather bleak, isn't it?"

"He didn't need much, as a man living on his own."

"Yes, with his crosswords to keep him company." Ettie went back to the crosswords on the countertop once more and when she picked up a page, she saw it was stuck to another one. When she pulled them apart, she saw a piece of candy. Kelly watched closely but didn't say anything more to her about not touching things. Then she opened a nearby jar and saw it was full of soft candies. Her gaze returned to the pages.

"You're fascinated by those, aren't you?" Elsa-May asked.

"I'm fascinated by the process he used."

"Apart from crosswords and charity work, what else do you know about Titus?" asked Kelly.

"Not a great deal. We weren't close with him. And now you know everything we know," Elsa-May gave a sharp nod.

"We'll take another look around." Ettie went to the far bedroom of the house and looked out the window. She was right; the white pebbles went the entire way around the house. And being as isolated as he was, he would've heard a car or a buggy coming toward him, or even someone on foot. He'd opened the door to someone, but who might it have been? Why would someone want him dead and out-of-the-way? When she sighed, the detective appeared at her shoulder.

"Who would have benefited from his death?" he asked.

"I would say his son would've benefited, financially."

"Which son? And for that matter, what about the wife, since they weren't divorced?"

"As I said before, with one son out of the community, he would've left everything to the son who stayed, Albie. As for Sophie, I don't think he would've left anything to her."

"We'll find out soon enough."

"How long will it take you to find that out?"

"Not long. Did Titus have a love interest?"

"He was still married, so if he did he wouldn't have been flaunting her, put it that way. It would've been a secret. That's forbidden."

"I wonder if the wife had her nose out of joint about something."

Ettie shrugged. "I wouldn't know. I haven't seen her since she left the community."

"It surprises me that you don't go to all the charity events."

"We've been to our share, but not lately, as I said earlier. As for Sophie, I never saw her at any of them."

"Very good."

Ettie had a last look around the bedroom and

walked out to the living room with him. There they found Elsa-May sitting down with pen in hand ready to write on something.

"Stop!" Kelly yelled out rushing toward her.

Elsa-May looked up at him with her reading glasses perched on her nose. "But I have a word. I'm sure it's right. It fits the space and starts with the correct letter."

"I asked you not to touch anything," Kelly snarled.

Ettie was shocked. He hadn't said anything stern to her when she touched the papers or the jar of candy in the kitchen.

"I haven't yet." Elsa-May opened her blue eyes wide, and Ettie said, "We should get going now."

"Already?" Elsa-May asked.

The detective's voice boomed. "Yes, I've got work to do and you ladies have to rest up today if you're going to the auction tomorrow."

Where has the nice and pleasant Detective Kelly gone? Ettie wondered.

CHAPTER 4

When Detective Kelly drove them back to the house, Ettie asked, "What time will you get there tomorrow?"

"I'm not sure yet. It just depends what tomorrow brings for me. I've got a ton of tedious paperwork and I'm the head of the major crime unit dealing with fugitives and gangs."

"It sounds like you've got a lot on your plate," Ettie said.

"You don't know the half of it."

"Did you get a promotion."

Kelly grunted and then they said their goodbyes and the two sisters walked to their house as Detective Kelly's car zoomed away.

"Why did you have to touch the crossword back at Titus's house? He told us not to touch anything."

"I didn't."

"You were just about to," Ettie said remembering Elsa-May had wanted to fill in a word.

"If they wanted any of those papers, they would've taken them already."

"You don't know that for certain."

"I suppose you're right. I just couldn't help myself. Just like you with the candy jar and the sticky papers. *Jah,* I saw you. I don't see why Kelly yelled at me, but not at you."

Ettie rolled her eyes and then pushed the door open. Before they got inside, Snowy darted between their legs and then stood on the top step staring after Detective Kelly's car.

"Look at him. He knew that was Detective Kelly in the car. He probably heard his voice."

"Jah, he seems to have a liking for him, for some reason."

"That makes two."

Ettie turned around to look at Elsa-May. "Two what?"

"Two beings who have a liking for Detective Kelly. Snowy and Kelly's new wife."

Ettie chuckled.

~

THE CHARITY FUNCTION was held in one of the large parks just past the town center. The money raised was going to the charity set up by Max Burley for the poor and the homeless in the area. It had been Titus's job to organize the Amish people to make and donate goods for the charity auction, and to organize the various stallholders for the day.

It was always the understanding that a percentage raised by the stallholders was given to the charity. The goods auctioned had been donated to the charity. At least, that was how Ettie and Elsa-May had been told things worked.

"It's going to be a long day," Ettie said to Elsa-May as they stepped out of the taxi.

"It will be if you don't stop complaining."

"Me?" Ettie said, thinking she was never one to complain.

"We don't have to stay all day. We'll just find out what we can about Titus and who wanted to kill him."

"It won't be that easy."

"I didn't say it was going to be easy."

Ettie was just about to suggest they split up and go their separate ways so they could double their efforts in the same amount of time, but didn't get a chance to speak before Betsy Jo was upon them. Betsy Jo was a young woman who had to know everything that was going on within their community.

"Have you heard about Titus?" Betsy Jo asked.

"Jah, we know," Ettie told her.

"What did you hear?" Elsa-May inquired.

"He was stabbed with a syringe, that's what I heard."

"Who told you?" Ettie asked.

"Everyone knows and everyone's talking about it. I didn't know if you knew as well."

Ettie fiddled with the strings of her *kapp.* If everyone knew, they just might overhear some information today that might be useful.

"I wonder who's going to take over from him organizing these charity events?" Betsy Jo said as she looked around the field.

"He didn't organize the events themselves," Elsa-May said.

"What part did he organize, then?" she asked.

"He organized the community members to donate things, and he organized the stalls."

"I know that. It was Max who did the rest of the work. I meant the part that he did. Who's going to take over that?"

"Betsy Jo, that's not what you said."

Betsy Jo shrugged.

Ettie's gaze swept along the double row of stalls.

Eighty percent of them were run by Amish folk. And that meant Titus would've done a lot of the work.

"Did you come to buy anything today?" Betsy Jo asked.

"We might buy a few things," Elsa-May said.

"Janie Beiler is here with her jams."

Ettie clapped her hands in excitement. They didn't make their own jams these days, and Janie made the best jams. "We should buy a couple of jars, Elsa-May."

"We will, before they all go. Where's her stall?"

Betsy Jo pointed them toward the stall, telling them it was at the other end of the field. "Oh, Maud has arrived. I must tell her about Titus." Without even saying goodbye, Betsy Jo ran off to spread the news about Titus.

"I think all we can get out of today is some bottles of jam. I don't know why Detective Kelly wanted us to come here at all."

Ettie said, "You never know. If everyone's talking about Titus, we should learn some things."

"Humph. I'd say the opposite would be true, for sure and for certain. We'll just keep our eyes and ears open for a while just to keep the detective happy and then we'll go home."

"Jah, we'll go home and make ourselves some jam sandwiches."

Elsa-May chuckled. "As long as Janie has some left by the time we get there."

Ettie said, "I'm walking as fast as I can."

"Is that as fast as you can go?"

"I'm conserving my energy, so I'll be able to last all day."

"This is as fast as I can go." Elsa-May took off walking at great speed.

"Stop, Elsa-May, you'll do yourself an injury."

Elsa-May stopped and waited for Ettie to catch up.

"I didn't know you could walk that fast."

"Walking every day with Snowy is keeping me fit. You should try it."

"I'm not overweight, so there's not much point to exercise."

"I'm not overweight either." Ettie didn't say a word, then Elsa-May added, "I admit I used to be, but I've lost a lot of weight. Don't you think so?"

"Maybe," Ettie said wishing the conversation would end. She couldn't tell a lie. She thought Elsa-May looked the same weight as she had several months ago when the doctor told her she should lose weight. Although she walked nearly every day, she ate twice as much.

"What do you mean by maybe? Can't you tell I've lost weight?"

"You possibly have, it's just ... I can't tell."

"You must need your eyesight checked, Ettie. I've lost a lot."

"Okay."

"Why can't you admit it? Do you think you can be the only skinny one in the household?"

"The goal is to be healthy, not skinny," Ettie pointed out, trying to shift the subject slightly, so she wouldn't have to tell Elsa-May she still hadn't lost weight.

Janie saw them heading to her store and she waved at them.

"She's smiling, so she must have some jam left."

"Good. I hope she has blackberry jam."

"And strawberry," Ettie added.

CHAPTER 5

When they were a few steps away from her stall, Janie stooped down and pulled some jam out of a box underneath the table. Then she placed two jars on top of the table. "I saved these last two jars for someone special. You can take them."

"What are they?" Ettie asked.

"Apricot jam and they're my last two jars."

"We'll take them!" Ettie said. "Along with …" Ettie smiled and looked at the assortment of jams and preserves on the trestle table. "Hmm, there's a lot to choose from."

Elsa-May nudged Ettie in the ribs. "Look, Ettie, blueberry."

"Ah, let's take a jar of blueberry. You choose the last one, Elsa-May."

Elsa-May reached out and picked up another jar. "Pear jam."

"Jah, that's lovely."

While Elsa-May was counting out her money and Janie was putting their four jams into a heavy paper bag, Ettie said, "I suppose you've heard about Titus, Janie?"

"Jah, it's tragic that he'd die so suddenly like that. He had such high hopes of Sophie coming back and they'd all be a happy family again. And if she came back, then Simon might come back too."

"I didn't know Titus had any communication with Sophie."

"It was Titus who told me that. He seemed to think there was a chance of Sophie and him reuniting. Anyway, I've probably said more than I should."

"That's okay," Elsa-May said. "We won't repeat anything." She handed over their change.

After they'd left Janie's stall, they spent some time asking around and listening to conversations to see what they could learn about Titus's murder.

After three hours, they hadn't heard any theories going around as to who might have killed him.

"This is a complete waste of time," Elsa-May whispered to Ettie.

"Nee it's not. We've got the jam."

At that moment, the loudspeaker squealed, and

then a deep voice announced that the auction was about to commence.

Elsa-May said, "There's no point in us staying for this. It will be too loud for anyone to talk and they'll just be selling things we don't need anyway."

"Okay. I would say we should go home, but we haven't found anything out."

"Well, that's Kelly's job, isn't it?" Elsa-May said.

"Jah, but ... Wait a moment, wasn't he supposed to be here?"

"Jah."

They looked around at the crowd of Amish and *Englischers* but there was no Detective Kelly.

"I wonder where he is?"

"Let's go home, then," Ettie said.

"Okay, but before we go, let's have a look at a couple of those candy stalls we saw." She swung around and faced Ettie. "Unless you think I'm too overweight?"

"You might get that way if you eat too much. Then all that walking you do in the mornings will be wasted. Remember what your doctor said?"

"Denke, Ettie. I remember what he said. He said I could have some sweet things in balanced moderation. Meaning, I can have a piece of candy now and again. I won't deprive myself. I'll go alone." Elsa-May turned and strode to the candy stalls.

Ettie had no choice but to follow, knowing that Elsa-May had never been able to stop at just one piece, but she wasn't brave enough to point that out.

While Elsa-May stocked up on candy, Ettie stood close by staring into the distance at Max Burley. She was disappointed that no announcement had been made of Titus's death, or how Titus had poured a great deal of effort into those charity events. Surely out of respect and gratefulness for Titus's many hours Max should've said something in acknowledgment.

And Max was the one who had found Titus, but there he was with a smile on his face as the auctioneer, standing next to him, sold off the first lot of goods. Max didn't look like a man who'd found a dead man two days before.

She wondered what Detective Kelly had found out about him, and that was going to be the first question she asked when she saw him again.

"Come on, Ettie."

Ettie looked over at Elsa-May, who clutched three paper bags full of candy.

"Are we ready to go?" Elsa-May asked.

"We'll have to go home now because neither of us can hold any more." Ettie had been charged with carrying the glass jars of jam, and they were getting heavy.

They walked to the side of the field where there were two waiting taxis.

They both got into the back seat and, as the taxi drove away, they caught a glimpse of Detective Kelly driving toward the park.

"There he is," Elsa-May said.

"He'll think we weren't here."

"Not much we can do about that now. We stayed for long enough. We can't wait around for him all day."

"Anyway, it's probably better that we weren't here when he was."

"That's true," Elsa-May said.

"Don't you think it's a little odd that Max Burley didn't say anything about Titus?"

"Nee. It wasn't a memorial service it was a charity auction. Many of the people there wouldn't have known who Titus was."

"Over half the people there were Amish, Elsa-May."

"And the other half weren't."

"So, you don't think it was funny that he didn't say a few words in acknowledgment? And he was smiling."

Elsa-May stared at her. "He's at a charity event. If he didn't have a pleasant look on his face people would wonder what was wrong. He has to smile."

"I still think he could've said a couple of words. It would've been nice." Ettie looked at the road ahead. There was just something about that Max Burley that she didn't like.

"He was the one who found Titus. You can't be suspicious of him, surely?"

"Did I say I was suspicious?"

"I know that look in your eyes," Elsa-May said.

Ettie cast her gaze downward. "I'm just thinking about things, that's all."

"You ladies talking about that Amish man that died the other day?" the taxi driver commented.

"Yes, how did you know?" Elsa-May asked.

"Just a good guess. I heard about him on the radio. I normally have the radio playing all day every day, not when I drive you Amish people somewhere."

"What did you hear exactly?" Ettie asked.

"Just he was found dead that's all, and he lived on a remote property somewhere. The police asked for help from the public. That's what they do when they've got no idea what's going on."

To Ettie, the driver was right. That meant Detective Kelly had no leads and no direction whatsoever, and that's why he'd come to them. That made perfect sense. The rest of the journey, Ettie and Elsa-May kept quiet, not wanting the driver to overhear any more than he already had.

When they got home, the first thing Ettie did was fill up the teakettle with water and then she placed it on the gas stove and lit the burner underneath it.

"Jam sandwich, Elsa-May?"

"Jah, please," she called out from her favorite chair in the living room.

Ettie hoped Elsa-May wasn't getting started into the candies already. Sometimes living with Elsa-May was like looking after a small child. There were better ways she could spend her time other than having to worry about her older sister's eating habits.

CHAPTER 6

The next day was Sunday and Ettie had half expected Kelly to stop by their house Saturday evening after the charity auction, but he hadn't.

The funeral was announced for Wednesday and that meant the body had been released already. They had to know the exact cause of death by now. The bishop went on to say that the viewing would be held at Albie's house.

After the meeting, Ettie made a beeline for Titus's son, Albie. "Albie, I'm so sorry to hear about your *vadder.*"

"Hi, Ettie. *Denke.* It was a huge shock."

"Do the police know anything more about who did it?"

"I don't know." He shook his head.

"Well, what happened?"

"Max Burley found him dead and that's all I want to say. I won't give you the dreadful details."

"Can I do anything to help out for Wednesday?"

"Nee, denke. It's all been taken care of."

"Okay. Let me know if there's anything at all I can do, will you?"

He slowly nodded and his lips turned upward slightly at the corners. "I will."

"Elsa-May is fascinated by your *vadder's* crosswords."

Albie nodded. "He loved his crosswords. It was pretty much like keeping a diary for him. They each had a theme. Did you ever notice that?"

"A theme?"

"Jah."

"What do you mean?"

"Whatever was going on in his life, he used that subject to create his crosswords around. Maybe I could tell because I was closest to him. We weren't that close, but no one was too friendly with him."

Ettie nodded, and then Albie's attention was taken by a swarm of people heading his way. "I'll talk to you later, Albie." She walked away wondering how she could find the latest crosswords his father had done. Then she'd know what had been on

Titus's mind the day he died. She hurried over to Elsa-May and told her what Albie had said.

"We've got to go back and have another look in the *haus*."

"Shall we ask Albie if that's okay?" Ettie asked.

"Nee, of course not," Elsa-May spat out.

"The detective?"

"Nee, of course not! We have to go there ourselves and tell no one."

"Break in?" Ettie asked.

"It won't be like that. Kelly let us in last time, but we didn't know what we were looking for."

"You were reading one of the crosswords. What was the word that Kelly stopped you from writing?"

"Hmm." Elsa-May tapped a finger on her chin. "It's on the tip of my tongue. I can't quite remember."

"Try harder."

"It'll come to me. It's no use. We'll have to go back there. Let's go now."

"Right now?" Ettie asked.

"Jah!"

"But the food's just coming out."

"We don't have time for food."

It was a surprise to hear Elsa-May say that.

"Come on, Ettie, it won't hurt us to miss one meal."

"I'm not worried. Let's walk up to the shanty and call for a taxi."

Elsa-May said, "And with everyone still here, no one will be going out to his *haus*."

Ettie and Elsa-May managed to slip away without being noticed and hurried up the road to the nearest shanty. The taxi arrived quickly and they had the driver take them right to the door of Titus's house.

Then Elsa-May whispered to Ettie, "Shall we have the taxi wait for us?"

"Nee. We don't know how long we'll be. Titus has a phone in his barn. He's got to have one."

"It might be disconnected by now."

Ettie leaned over to the driver. "Is there any chance you can organize a taxi to collect us from here in half an hour?"

"Sure."

Now that they had that arranged, they paid the driver and got out of the car. When the taxi drove away, they realized they were faced with a locked front door.

"What are we going to do now?" Elsa-May asked.

"Try a window." They walked over the crunchy white pebbles and then they found a window with a lock that was loose. Ettie jiggled it until the lock released. "Got it."

"Well go on. Get in."

"Me?" Ettie said.

"Jah, you."

"You'll need to give me a leg up."

Elsa-May did just that and Ettie managed to climb in the window. Her prayer *kapp* fell off in the process and her dress got snagged on a nail protruding from the window frame, but at least she was in. She picked up her *kapp* and placed it back on her head. Then she looked at her dress and saw it had a hole. "Oh, bother." Then she opened the front door for Elsa-May.

"Who were you talking to just now? Is there someone here?"

"Just myself. My dress got ripped." She held it up and showed Elsa-May.

"Just patch it. It'll be fine."

"I'm not going to patch it. That'll look dreadful. The whole dress is ruined." Ettie pouted as she stared at the jagged hole.

"Patch it. Don't be so vain."

"I'm not vain. You only patch boy's pants or work clothes, you don't patch good dresses."

"Of course, you do."

"You wouldn't patch a good dress, but you expect me to?"

"Patch it and use it as a *haus* dress. Now no more

talk about it." Elsa-May placed her hands on her hips and stared at her as only a big sister could.

"I'll toss it in the trash. I've got plenty of *haus* dresses."

"Are you going to throw away a perfectly good dress over one little rip? What would *Dat* say?"

Ettie pressed her lips tightly together. Their father would've said to patch the dress. "Forget it!"

"You can barely notice it anyway."

When they walked into the kitchen, they stopped in shock. The entire place was bare.

"Elsa-May, they've gone. All the paper that was on the countertop last time has gone, along with the dictionary."

"I can see that much for myself. The question is, who took them? Would it have been Titus's family, or the detective?"

"It might have been Titus's family doing some cleaning up."

Elsa-May said, "And they would've thought all the paper spread across the table was rubbish."

"Maybe it was, but just maybe it wasn't."

"Should we find out what happened to it?" Elsa-May asked.

Ettie stared at Elsa-May. "What do you suggest we do? Tell Albie we broke into his *vadder's haus* and we're upset because the papers are missing and then ask him who took them?"

Elsa-May pulled a face. "I suppose that's out of the question."

"And we can't say anything to the detective."

"Nee, not directly, but we can tell the detective what Janie said."

Ettie sighed. "Now we've got ages to wait for the taxi."

"It's better than walking miles to call for one."

"I guess so."

"What's that?" Elsa-May asked.

Ettie heard a car and then they both hurried to look out the window. "Who could that be?"

"It's Sophie."

"We can't let her find us here."

"Why is she here, I wonder?"

Ettie said, "We'll have to hide somewhere."

"We can't."

"We can and we will. She won't be happy to find us here, uninvited—common trespassers."

"We're trespassing?" Elsa-May asked.

"Jah, and probably breaking all kinds of laws by being in her ex-husband's *haus.*"

"They were never divorced."

"Quick!" Ettie grabbed Elsa-May's sleeve and

hustled her to the spare room. There was a two-door closet and she pushed Elsa-May in and then stepped in beside her, and then closed the doors. They had slats so the sisters could see through them into the room.

"Will she be able to see us in here?" Elsa-May whispered.

"Nee, no one can see in."

"What if she's here to find something? She might look in here."

Ettie hissed, "We'll have to pray she doesn't."

"Gott might not answer our prayers since we just did a break and enter."

"Elsa-May, it was only for the best intentions." Then they heard a key jiggle in the lock. "Sh." Ettie dug Elsa-May in the ribs.

"Ow."

"Shush."

They listened hard and heard high heels clicking along the floorboards. Then they heard sounds of her opening and closing the kitchen cupboards. After that, the heels clicked off to the bedroom. They heard doors open and a few minutes later they were closed. Then they saw her enter the spare room where they were. She looked under the bed, and then she lifted the mattress. After that, she stood there with her hands on her hips looking around. Her eyes flew to a chest of drawers and then she opened and closed each drawer. From the speed she was opening and closing them, the drawers must have all been empty.

Then her gaze traveled to the closet in which they were hiding. Ettie held her breath and Elsa-May clutched her arm in near-panic. They were about to be discovered. All kinds of excuses ran through Ettie's head. What would they say they were doing in the closet? No excuse sounded reasonable. She had to suppress an urge to laugh as she imagined Sophie's shocked expression when she saw them. Then music rang through the air and Sophie reached into the back pocket of her jeans and pulled out a cell phone.

"Yeah? No nothing. There's nothing here. The place has been cleaned out. I'm coming back now." She shoved the cell phone back into her pocket and left the room.

A minute later, they heard the front door shut and the car door open and close, and then her car's engine started. Ettie looked over at Elsa-May to see her eyes shut tightly. "She's going," Ettie whispered.

"Sh. Don't say anything until we hear the car leave."

When the car had driven away, they opened the closet door.

"I've never been so scared in all my born days,"

Elsa-May wiped her forehead. "I'm sweating. What if she killed him and was coming back for something she'd forgotten?"

"It's possible I suppose."

"What could she have been looking for?"

"I've got no idea. We'll most likely see her at the funeral and we can talk to her then," Ettie said.

"And are we going to ask her what she was looking for when we saw her from within her dead husband's closet?" Elsa-May asked sarcastically.

"*Nee*, but we can perhaps get some idea about her. We don't even know if she left the marriage on bad terms or on good terms with Titus. I don't know what else we can do."

"She left the community too, so I'd say she left on bad terms. Let's have a look around to see if she overlooked anything."

They both looked through the house but didn't find anything. Titus's estranged wife was right; the house had been cleaned out. Who had she been talking to on the phone?

When the taxi arrived, they hurried out of the house in case anyone else might arrive and catch them.

CHAPTER 7

That afternoon, Ettie heated up leftovers of roasted chicken and roasted vegetables. If she kept Elsa-May filled up on good food, she'd be less likely to eat so many jam sandwiches. Perhaps it would've been better if they hadn't gone to that auction.

Soon after they had finished the meal that night, Detective Kelly arrived. Elsa-May closed Snowy out in the backyard before they let Kelly in the door.

Once they were all seated, Ettie asked, "Have you found out anything?"

"I came to ask you that."

"We expected to see you at the auction," Elsa-May said.

"I was there."

"We didn't see you."

Ettie realized Elsa-May had forgotten they'd seen him when they were leaving.

"I was there," Kelly repeated.

"We left early. I suppose that's why we didn't see you," Ettie said, not wanting to point out Elsa-May's forgetfulness.

Kelly ignored Ettie's comment. "How close was Titus to this Max Burley who ran the charity?"

Ettie and Elsa-May looked at one another.

"We don't know," Elsa-May said.

"Would you be able to find that out?" he asked.

They nodded and he sniffed the air. "That food smells delicious."

"Ettie cooked a roast."

"I only heated up leftovers, but there's plenty left if you'd like some."

"No thanks. My wife is keeping my dinner hot." He gave a self-satisfied grin.

"What's her name?" Ettie asked.

"Cynthia."

"That's a lovely name."

"She's a lovely woman." His face lit up as he spoke of her. "Now back to the reason I came here. If you could find out about the relationship that Titus had with Max, I'd appreciate it."

"All we know is that they worked closely. Max and his wife, Terese, have been doing these charity events for years. They must've raised a ton of money."

The detective nodded. "It might interest you to know that the charity is being investigated by the IRS."

"Really?"

The detective nodded. "Yes. But that doesn't mean they're guilty of anything, of course. I'm just saying they're being investigated."

"But they might be guilty of something?" Elsa-May commented.

"It's a possibility."

"And if they've been doing the wrong thing, it might be possible that Titus found out about it and wasn't happy," Ettie said.

"Maybe he threatened to expose them," Elsa-May suggested.

"Possibly, but just keep that information to yourselves for the moment."

"*Jah,* of course, we will. We'll be at Titus's funeral on Wednesday."

"What do you know about his ex-wife?" Ettie asked.

"Current wife. They're only separated," Elsa-May corrected Ettie.

Ettie stared at Elsa-May, "I didn't say divorced."

Kelly answered, "She's of interest to us, as are all his close friends and family."

"Is she in a new relationship?" Ettie asked.

"She has a neighbor she spends a lot of time with. He conveniently lives right next door. Why do you ask?" He looked from Ettie to Elsa-May.

Elsa-May was the one to answer. "It's nothing. We haven't talked to her since she left, so we just wondered, that's all."

"We'll talk to her at the funeral," Ettie said.

"Do that and see what you can find out."

"You would've talked to her by now, wouldn't you?" Elsa-May asked.

"I said I did. I've talked to everyone, but we're no further ahead."

"Did you go back to the house and take anything else out?" Elsa-May asked the detective.

Ettie stared at her not believing her ears.

"No. Why?"

"Oh nothing. I was just wondering."

"You must've asked for a reason," Kelly said.

"No."

Ettie had to intervene. "Are you sure you wouldn't like something to eat, Detective?"

"No. I must get home. I don't want to upset the wife. I told her I was on my way."

Ettie had never liked men referring to their wives

as 'the wife.' "I hope we can meet Cynthia some time."

He raised his eyebrows. "Maybe."

"Is there anything in particular you'd like us to find out for you?" Elsa-May asked him. "I feel like there is but you're not saying it."

"Just like I said, I'd like you to find out how close he was to the ... Max and his wife, Terese."

Elsa-May nodded. "Okay."

Ettie pushed herself to her feet. "Perhaps you can stay longer another time."

Kelly stood up. "If I don't see you before, I'll stop by the night of the funeral in case you find out something useful. Call if you learn anything before that."

"We will." Ettie walked him to the door while Elsa-May stayed sitting. When Ettie closed the door, she walked back and sat down on the couch and stared at Elsa-May. "What did you have to mention the house for? That was silly."

"I just wanted to know if he took anything out of it because if he didn't, someone else did."

"*Jah*, probably Titus's son, either one of his sons, and they had every right to. Kelly said himself that his investigators, or forensic people, were finished there. He said that on the day he took us through."

"Okay. Well, I didn't think of that." Elsa-May picked up her knitting and started.

"I'll let Snowy back in." When Ettie leaned down and unlocked the dog door, Snowy scampered through the door, and then sniffed around where the detective had been. "We need Snowy on the job," Ettie said. "Snowy would be able to sniff out the killer."

"They sometimes use sniffer dogs."

"Only for missing people, I think. I wonder what the funeral will reveal."

"Probably nothing."

"So, Sophie has taken up with her neighbor. That's interesting. I wonder if that's who she was speaking to on her cell phone," Ettie said.

"More importantly, what was she looking for?"

CHAPTER 8

Wednesday came, the day of the funeral, and Elsa-May's grandson, Jeremiah, picked up Ettie and Elsa-May. His wife, Ava, was away visiting relatives.

"Denke for collecting us, Jeremiah," Ettie said.

"Glad to."

Ettie and Elsa-May knew they would have to be careful what they said around Jeremiah because he was very much against anything he considered gossiping. Ettie recognized their father's personality in Jeremiah.

"It's a lovely day," Ettie said.

"It's warm for this time of year," Jeremiah commented. "Feels nice."

"When does Ava get back from visiting her cousin?" Ettie asked.

"Next week."

"You must miss her," Elsa-May said.

"I do. We've never really been apart like this since we were married." When they arrived at Albie's house, Jeremiah said, "Let me know when you want to leave today. If you get weary, I'll take you home."

"Denke. We should be okay," Elsa-May said.

First, there would be the viewing of Titus at Albie's house and then the buggy procession to the graveyard. After the burial, everyone would return to Albie's house for light refreshments.

When they'd gotten out of the buggy and were walking to the house for the viewing, Ettie noticed that Elsa-May had something clutched in her hand.

"What's that?" Ettie asked.

Elsa-May moved her hand under the edge of her apron. "What?"

"What have you got in your hand?"

She moved her hand back to the front and opened it slightly to reveal a folded piece of paper.

"What is it?"

Elsa-May whispered, "It's a crossword."

"Why did you bring it?"

"I'm going to slip it into his coffin with him."

Ettie gasped. "You can't do that."

"Why not?"

"Is it one of his crosswords?"

"Naturally. I wouldn't be putting someone else's crossword in his coffin with him, would I?"

Ettie could scarcely believe her ears. From the wooden look on her sister's face, she knew Elsa-May was serious. "You're just impossible. You better make sure no one sees you."

"They won't. Don't worry, I've got it all figured out. I'll put my hand up to the coffin when I'm looking down at him, and I'll let my hand rest on the edge of the coffin. The paper will just slip into the coffin down the side. No one will see it."

"You better hope not."

"Will it really matter?"

"It could. You'll embarrass yourself if someone sees it. You're not a member of his family, so you've really got no say in what goes into his coffin—if anything."

"I don't think any of his family really understood him. He wasn't that close to Albie, and he lived out there on his lonesome with just his words to occupy his mind."

"How do you know he wasn't close to Albie? They seemed to get along."

"Titus wasn't living with him. They weren't living together. Albie never married. It would've made sense if the two of them moved in together. Just like we did."

Ettie frowned. "We're close to our *kinner*, but we don't live with them."

"We have many children and Albie only had the two boys. Now that Simon's left us, he's only got Albie."

"Still, what you said doesn't make sense. He might've liked living by himself."

"I don't want to argue," Elsa-May said.

Neither did Ettie, she was just trying to make her sister see sense. For the sake of peace, she agreed with her. "You could be right. He had his charities and his crosswords."

"The charity functions weren't held all year around, though."

"Let's just get inside, shall we?"

"After you," Elsa-May said.

Ettie stepped through the door first and saw Albie standing at the front of the room near the coffin. Not everybody had arrived yet. Jeremiah had a habit of being early.

"Now's my chance," whispered Elsa-May as she charged ahead of Ettie.

Ettie's heart pounded, hoping Elsa-May wouldn't be caught enacting her kind-hearted but stupid idea.

She was acting like a child, not like a woman in her eighties.

It wasn't as though Titus was there in his body, she reminded herself. The part of him that lay in the coffin was just his shell. He was at home with God, so what good would a crossword do him? This little scheme showed Ettie that Elsa-May was sentimental, and not nearly as coldly practical as she seemed.

Elsa-May greeted Albie and said a few kind words and just as Ettie was doing the same, she saw out of the corner of her eye that Elsa-May's plan was unfolding. Elsa-May put her hand up to the coffin and then looked in, but to Ettie's horror, she saw the piece of paper fall to the floor. She didn't know where to look. Out of the corner of her eye, she saw Elsa-May bend over to pick it up.

When Albie looked at what Elsa-May was doing, Ettie stepped in between them, and asked, "And will your *mudder* be coming today, Albie?"

Thankfully, that took Albie's attention off Elsa-May. Now with her back to her older sister, Ettie couldn't see what she was doing and she hoped that nobody else could see either.

"She said she wouldn't come, but she might still show up."

"You've been in contact with her then?"

He nodded. "She visits me every few months."

"I see. It would be nice to see her again. Where is she living nowadays?"

"She lives in town. Right next door to her candle shop on the road behind the farmers market."

"Oh really?"

He nodded.

"I've seen a candle shop there. No one ever mentioned she owned it."

"She just took it over last week, but she's lived next door to it for a long time."

"That explains it." The rumor mill was slow that week with Titus's death taking everyone's attention. "So, she bought it around the time of your *vadder's* death?"

"That's right. A little before that, I guess."

When Ettie noticed more people coming up to speak to Albie, she moved away, and Elsa-May was right by her side.

"Did you do it?" Ettie whispered.

"*Jah*, just like I planned it."

"Not exactly like you planned it. I saw the paper land on the floor."

Elsa-May chortled. "I finally managed to slip it into the coffin right between his arm and the wall of the coffin."

"Oh, you didn't put it in his hand along with a pen?"

"Don't be silly, Ettie, it wouldn't be any fun for him to do a crossword that he himself created. He'd know the answers."

Ettie rolled her eyes. She had no reply for that.

CHAPTER 9

When they got out of Jeremiah's buggy at the graveyard, Ettie saw some *Englischers* she didn't know. As they walked over to the freshly dug grave, Ettie whispered to Elsa-May, "Who's that talking to Simon?"

"How would I know?"

"I thought you knew everything."

Elsa-May smiled. "I mostly do, but I've never seen those people before. Wait a minute, *jah,* I have. I saw them at the auction. He's the man who runs the charity, right?"

Ettie nodded. "You're right, that's Max Burley. I didn't recognize him at first in a suit. And that's his wife in the pink hat."

"I would assume so."

"I thought *Englischers* wore black to funerals.

Pink's a little bright for a funeral don't you think?" Ettie asked.

"I don't think it matters."

"You don't think she's trying to send a message?"

"A message about what and to whom?" Elsa-May looked down her nose at Ettie.

"To us Amish people that she doesn't care about Titus."

"That's ridiculous, Ettie. If she didn't care about Titus why would she be here?"

"I can think of half a dozen reasons off the top of my head."

"Do me a favor and don't tell me what they are."

Ettie kept walking and looked around the crowd that had gathered around the grave. There were the bishop and his wife talking to Albie, and now Simon was by himself on the other side. Mostly, at funerals family stood together but then again Albie was still in the community and Simon had left years ago. And where was their mother? She hadn't even bothered to show up.

Elsa-May grabbed a hold of Ettie's arm.

"Easy, you just nearly pulled me over."

"I nearly slipped that's why. I grabbed hold of you so I wouldn't fall."

"Well, don't do it again or we'll both end up toppling over." Ettie pulled her arm away. And then felt mean for being short tempered with her sister. She didn't like it when Elsa-May was that way with her. "I'm sorry, Elsa-May. I'm just trying to figure this whole thing out and you gave me a fright. I didn't mean to react like that."

"That's okay, I'm used to it."

Ettie's mouth dropped open and she stood still, and without missing a beat Elsa-May kept walking. Throughout the bishop's sermon at the graveside, Ettie watched the reactions of the two brothers. Albie had a blank stare, looking at his father's coffin about to be lowered into the grave, and Simon was staring at Albie, looking none too pleased.

Then Ettie looked around to see who else was there. She remembered a detective telling her long ago that he always kept an eye on people who came to funerals. Often times the murderer came. Her first thought was it might be someone in Titus's immediate family—one of the two boys or his estranged wife.

Then there were the two people who worked with the charity; Max, the man who ran it, and his wife, Terese. Ettie made up her mind to talk to Max and Terese once the funeral was over. She could get talking to them and offer her services and that way she might also find out exactly what Titus had been doing.

Most of the community was there and also visitors from outside. As her eyes swept over the crowd, she wondered who would want Titus dead. Was it a crime of greed, hate, or love? She knew they were the most common reasons for murder along with revenge. For convenience sake, she ruled out a love tryst because of Titus's age and besides, he was already married and wouldn't be able to marry again unless he left the community and got a divorce.

Then again, maybe his wife wanted to be free of him and maybe she was due to get some money from his estate. Ettie made a mental note, planning to visit Sophie in the next couple of days.

The bishop gave his usual short talk on life and death, and the cycle of life. He explained how love of God and love toward our fellow man was the most important thing in life. It made sense. Funerals were always a good time for people to get their lives in perspective. Life was so short, and it often helped to be reminded of that.

Ettie shed a tear as the coffin was lowered into the ground. She felt sorry for Titus sitting there keeping himself amused by his word puzzles and then his life was unexpectedly snatched away from him. She was sure he probably had things he still had wanted to do with his life—things he hadn't yet completed and now he would never have a chance to get them done.

"Come on, Ettie. What are you doing?"

Ettie looked across at Elsa-May and saw that nearly everybody had moved away. "I'm just thinking about poor old Titus. He didn't have a choice in this."

"People don't usually have a choice when they die."

"You know what I mean. He didn't have a chance to get his life in order before everything cruelly ended for him. That wasn't right." She stared down at the grave wondering why she was so affected by Titus's death. They hadn't even been close with him.

"You're just being dramatic. I think they call that a second childhood. You were like this when you were a young girl. You made a big deal out of everything. Everything was such a drama."

Ettie pointed to herself. "Me? I can remember someone just like that and it wasn't me."

Elsa-May put her hands on her hips. "I hope you don't mean it was me."

"I can remember you shouting at *Dat* when you couldn't get your way." It had only been once or maybe twice, but her being the eldest, the younger siblings couldn't believe what they heard coming out of Elsa-May's mouth.

Elsa-May lowered her head. Her voice softened. "We had very different ideas about things. I wanted to go to school beyond the eighth grade and he said education led to vanity and pride."

"He said it leads to pride, but I don't think he said vanity. Anyway, you did what you wanted. No one else in the family has ever reached your level of education."

"I know, but I regret the way I did it. I shouldn't have been disrespectful and raised my voice."

Elsa-May looked so sad that Ettie felt bad for bringing the whole thing up. "Never mind, we've all done things we regret."

Elsa-May nodded. "We better get back to Jeremiah's buggy. You know how cross he gets when we're late."

"Do you feel up to going back to Albie's *haus* for the refreshments? If you don't, we'll have Jeremiah take us home."

"I'm fine." Just as Elsa-May spoke, their attention was drawn by a loud argument that had broken out. They looked up to see Simon raising his voice at Albie, and as he spoke, his hands were flailing about in the air.

Everyone ignored the two men and headed toward their buggies with their backs turned.

"What are they arguing about, Ettie?"

"I can't quite hear." When Ettie and Elsa-May climbed into Jeremiah's buggy, Ettie asked, "What's going on?"

Jeremiah drew his eyebrows together. "I don't know. The only thing I know is that Albie is thinking of selling his *vadder's* property and he won't sell to Simon."

"So, the farm was left to Albie alone?" Elsa-May asked.

"That's right."

That's exactly what the sisters had expected. Everyone waited in their buggies until Albie got into his and then they followed Albie to his house.

Ettie didn't say any more to Jeremiah because she knew he didn't like to talk about people. But she was sure going to ask a few questions of people when she got to Albie's house.

CHAPTER 10

Albie had many of the ladies helping him with the food that day. He was the oldest of Titus's two sons and had never married. He lived alone in his small house and worked helping one of his neighbors on their farm.

When they arrived, Ettie made a beeline for Auntie Agnes as she saw her walking away from a group of people. The woman was a little younger than Ettie, but not by much. Everyone in the community called her Aunt Agnes and more often than not, she was a reliable source of information.

"Agnes,"

Agnes turned around to face her. She was a small woman, slightly stooped over, with brown eyes that looked far too large for her face. "Hello, Ettie. How are you today?"

"I have a bit of a cold hanging around, but other than that I'm good. What about yourself?"

"Did you see that argument between Titus's boys back at the cemetery?"

"I did, and it was terrible. The bishop was just staring at them not knowing what to do."

"I know."

Ettie asked, "Do you know what they were arguing about?"

"I do. Albie wants to sell the farm and Simon wants it. But Simon doesn't want to pay what it's worth. That's what I heard."

"Why does Albie want to sell it? I thought he'd want to make something of the farm—grow something on it. Because he's a farmer." Ettie shrugged her shoulders. "That's what I thought he'd do."

"Nee. He's happy with what he's doing now, helping out Frank a few days a week. That gives him enough money to live on."

"I did hear someone say that he doesn't want to sell it to his brother," Ettie said.

"That's right. He doesn't want to sell it to Simon because he said he's been offered a lot of money from someone else."

"Who?"

"The neighbor from the other side of Titus. He grows soybeans and wants to increase his acreage.

He's been at Titus to sell it to him for years. Titus wasn't using the land but because he didn't like the neighbor, he doggedly wouldn't sell to him." Aunt Agnes grinned.

"Oh, really?"

Aunt Agnes nodded. "It's true."

"I don't doubt it. And who is the neighbor?" Ettie asked, figuring she was stretching her luck.

"Billy Wilkes."

"Billy Wilkes. That name sounds familiar."

"He likes to be called Bill now that he's grown up."

"Were his parents William and Ida Wilkes?"

"That's right."

"I remember Billy now—a tall skinny boy with freckles and dark hair."

"That's him. Ida and William died in that dreadful buggy accident."

The memory came back to Ettie. "That was some time ago."

Agnes nodded.

"And Billy and Titus didn't get along?"

"They didn't. And I'm not sure why."

Ettie didn't know if that mattered or not, but she was sure going to store that in her memory banks for later. "That's interesting, Agnes, *denke.*"

"Who do you think killed him, Ettie?"

"I wouldn't know."

"Take a guess."

"I wouldn't like to, not until I have all the information. Who do you think killed him?"

"I wouldn't be surprised if it was Sophie," Agnes said.

"Surely not! She doesn't seem the type."

"What about that man over there? I don't like the look of him."

Maybe Agnes was losing her mind. Ettie looked over to where Agnes was pointing. It was Max talking with the bishop. Ettie wondered if Aunt Agnes just said that because he was an *Englischer*. Of course Ettie didn't have a good impression of Max, either.

It was time to move on. "I better go and say a few words to Albie," Ettie said.

"Very well. We must catch up properly. Why don't you and Elsa-May stop by sometime? One day soon?"

"*Jah*, we will."

It surprised Ettie that Simon had gone to his father's funeral, argued so loudly with Albie, and then left. It was also a shame that Sophie hadn't come, but Ettie couldn't really blame her for not coming to her husband's funeral. She would've felt awkward amongst the folk she'd left behind.

It must've been a disappointment to Simon that his father had left everything to Albie. Elsa-May and Ettie's father had left everything to their brothers. The girls in the family hadn't gotten anything. Even knowing what her father thought, that since his daughters were all married, they were already being taken care of, a little part of Ettie was still hurt. It was the thought of the matter rather than the money that was the issue.

And if what she was being told was true, it seemed quite unfair of Albie not to allow Simon to purchase the land and the home where he'd grown up. She couldn't blame Simon for being upset, although he ought to pay his brother a fair price. She wondered what Sophie thought about the whole thing. Perhaps there was more to the reason Albie wanted to sell his father's property to Billy Wilkes rather than to his own brother. Ettie made another mental note—they'd visit Billy too.

When Ettie looked for Elsa-May to tell her they would be visiting Sophie and also Billy Wilkes the very next day, she was surprised to see her already talking to Max and Terese. She hurried over to be involved in the conversation.

Elsa-May turned around to look at Ettie. "Ettie, have you met Max and his wife Terese?"

"No, I haven't."

Elsa-May introduced Ettie to them.

"I understand that Titus did a lot of work for you," Ettie said.

"He did a tremendous amount," Max said.

"I don't know what we'll do without him now," Terese said.

"And what exactly did he do for you?" Ettie asked.

Terese said, "He organized your community to pitch in with the fund-raising."

"He'd really do anything we asked him to do," Max added.

"And did you start the charity?" Ettie asked.

"I started it when I was a young man, after I heard my uncle's story. I didn't meet him until later in life. He'd been living on the streets for fifteen years. He'd been a highly educated man and fell onto rough times and wasn't able to get himself out of the rut he was in. And I didn't want that to happen to other people. It could really happen to anyone. Most people are only three months away from being homeless."

Elsa-May's eyes open widely. "Really?"

"Yes, it's true. Anything can happen at any time."

Ettie wondered if Max and his wife were hoping that Titus had left his estate to charity—their charity. She didn't like being so cynical, but she accepted it as just the way she was. She politely moved away from them, leaving Max and Terese talking to Elsa-May. Behind their pleasant faces and smiling eyes, Ettie was certain there was more to them, maybe even something sinister.

She waited behind the people that Albie was talking to so she could get a chance to say a word to him. A few minutes later, her chance came.

"Hello, Ettie. I suppose you heard that scene at the graveyard?"

"Oh, don't worry about that. Family members get irritated with each other sometimes. Even Elsa-May and I don't get along well some of the time. Are you moving into your *vadder's* property?"

He shook his head. "I'm selling it."

"Oh, I thought you would want to keep it. It used to be such good farming land back a few years ago."

"And it will be again. My *vadder's* neighbor grows soybeans and has always been looking for new land to enlarge his crop. I'm selling it to him."

"And you're staying on where you are?"

"That's right. My place suits me just fine."

"Are the police any further ahead finding out who did this to your *vadder?*"

"Nee." He shook his head.

"I see. I'm sorry for the sadness of it all."

"Jah, it was a shock."

"Speaking of shocks, I'm surprised your *mudder* isn't here. I thought I'd visit her tomorrow, do you think she would mind that?"

"I think she would like that, Ettie. I think she would like that very much. She wanted to come, but she and *Dat*—"

"I can understand. It'd be very awkward for her."

They were interrupted by people coming over to talk with Albie, and Ettie patted his arm gently and took her leave. She was pleased that she'd gotten to talk with him as much as she had.

She hurried back to Elsa-May who was by herself, having finished speaking with Max and Terese.

"Where have you been, Ettie?"

"I was talking to Albie."

"Did he say anything?"

"Not really. I thought we should visit his mother tomorrow and also …" Ette tapped a finger on her left side of her forehead. "There was someone else I wanted to visit, but it's completely left my mind. Let's see now... Oh yes, Billy Wilkes. He lives next door to Titus's place."

"Where's Billy been?"

"Elsa-May, he left the community years ago."

"Did he? Come to think of it I haven't seen him for a while."

Ettie shook her head at her sister. "Billy Wilkes is buying Titus's land from Albie. We'll visit Billy first, and then we'll go on to visit Sophie."

"Good idea."

Ettie tapped the side of her head. "Always thinking."

Elsa-May chuckled.

"Well, did you find out anything useful from Max and his wife?"

"Nothing."

"I feel there's something wrong with them, like they are not what they seem."

"I know what you mean. I felt like they were salespeople. All smiling to your face while they're thinking something quite different."

"Exactly," Ettie was glad her sister agreed with her. "They say all the right things, but their eyes seem cold."

CHAPTER 11

Aunt Agnes ran over to Ettie and tugged on her sleeve.

"What is it, Agnes?"

"I just heard something I thought you might be interested in."

"Jah?"

"Someone said that Billy Wilkes has always been asking Titus to sell to him since forever. I didn't know that, and now Albie said he'd sell the property to him. His *vadder* wouldn't be happy."

Aunt Agnes didn't remember she'd already told Ettie that, so Ettie figured she'd humor her. "That is interesting."

"Also … and listen closely because this is the most important thing I've got to tell you."

Ettie moved a little closer to her, wondering if

what Aunt Agnes was about to say was going to be just idle gossip, another repeated tidbit, or something of vital importance.

"I have heard that Sophie was there at Titus's home the night he died."

A shiver went down Ettie's spine. "That's odd. Where did you hear that?"

"I'm not sure now."

"What was she doing there?"

"I don't know, but she was seen."

"Do you think that's true?" Elsa-May asked.

Aunt Agnes took a step back. "I believe it. The person who told me is not one to lie about things."

"I didn't think anybody would be lying, but sometimes it's easy to make mistakes about these things."

Aunt Agnes frowned at Elsa-May. "There is no mistake about it. Sophie was at his *haus* the night he died."

Elsa-May turned away and started talking to someone else.

Meanwhile, Ettie wondered if Kelly already knew of Sophie's whereabouts that night. Had Sophie lied to Kelly? Kelly hadn't mentioned anyone known to have been at the house, other than Max who'd found Titus the next morning. If Sophie hadn't said anything, no one in the community would've told him. The Amish were never forthcoming with things like that. She looked back at Agnes, who was still standing there. "Do you have any idea who killed Titus?"

"No idea, and I'm not saying that Sophie had anything to do with his death, but how about the timing?" Aunt Agnes raised her eyebrows.

"It's funny you mention Sophie just now because I'm off to visit her tomorrow. Not by myself, I'm taking Elsa-May with me."

"That's a good idea, Ettie. Mind if I tag along?"

Ettie regretted opening her big mouth. "We're not sure what time we're going."

"Just as well I've got all day free, then."

"We'll see how things go. Elsa-May hasn't been feeling too well lately. She's had a problem with her ears." That was the best Ettie could come up with at short notice. It would be the very worst thing if they took Aunt Agnes with them because Sophie would remember what a gossip Aunt Agnes was and she wouldn't tell them anything.

"So, you might not be going?"

"I said I plan to go, but sometimes not everything works out to plan."

"If you do decide to go, stop by my house and collect me. I would love to see how she is."

Ettie nodded and then Elsa-May finished talking and turned back to face them.

Aunt Agnes said, "Elsa-May, I've heard you've not been well."

"I've been fine."

"Ettie said you've been ill."

They both stared at Ettie.

"I was just explaining to Agnes that we might see Sophie tomorrow and then again we might not. It all depends on how you're feeling. Agnes said she would go with us when we visit her."

Elsa-May put a hand to her head. "From time to time I haven't been feeling too well. So far, today's a good day."

"And the other day it was your ears giving you trouble, wasn't it, Elsa-May?"

Elsa-May nodded. "I had to go to the doctor."

"You should stay home and look after yourself more."

"I will, *jah*, I will."

Ettie put a hand on Agnes's arm. "If you'll excuse me there's someone I see that I need to talk to." Ettie made a hasty retreat. She knew Elsa-May was going to blame her for putting her on the spot, but it would be certain disaster to take Aunt Agnes with them. Or at least a totally wasted trip.

CHAPTER 12

After Jeremiah had dropped Ettie and Elsa-May at their home, they walked into their small living room. Elsa-May sat in her usual chair and Ettie sat on her couch. They exchanged the information that they had gleaned from the people at the funeral, and reviewed what they'd heard while they were together.

Ettie said, "The plan is to visit Billy Wilkes first tomorrow, and then from there we'll go on to Sophie's, okay?"

"*Jah*, you said that before. It sounds good. We'll do that." Elsa-May patted her stomach. "I don't think we'll need to eat tonight. In between all the talking, I did a lot of eating."

"I certainly won't eat tonight. I've had more than

enough. We could have an early night and then make an early start of it tomorrow."

"Where will we find Billy Wilkes?"

"He lives right next door to Titus. I told you that." Ettie frowned.

"Oh, that's right. I did hear that. I hope we can find out who killed Titus. What if someone else gets killed, too?"

"It hasn't happened yet."

"That's not much comfort." Elsa-May pulled out her knitting from the bag by her feet and popped her glasses onto her nose.

Ettie leaned forward and picked up Snowy who was pawing at the couch trying to get up. Snowy quickly made himself comfortable with his head and front paws on Ettie's lap. After a while of stroking his soft fur, Ettie's eyes slowly closed.

Just as the elderly sisters were dropping off to sleep after their big day, a loud knock sounded on their door. Snowy jumped off the couch barking, and ran up and down the room.

"Grab him, Elsa-May."

"I can't. I've dropped a stitch." Elsa-May pushed her glasses further up her nose and studied her knitting. "Don't worry. I might be able to fix it." She leaned into her bag and grabbed a crochet hook.

"There's someone at the door." Ettie managed to

grab Snowy, and then she put him outside and clipped the dog door shut. Then she opened the front door to see a smiling Detective Kelly.

"Ah, I've got it," Elsa-May yelled out.

Kelly frowned quizzically, and Ettie told him, "She dropped a stitch."

"Oh no."

"It's okay, she's picked it up again."

He chuckled in a good-natured manner. "Good."

"Come in," Ettie said.

He slowly walked inside. "I said I was stopping by after the funeral. I wanted you to find out how close Max and Terese were to Titus. Did you forget I was coming?"

"Did you, Ettie?" Elsa-May asked from her seated position.

Ettie stifled a yawn. "Did you, Elsa-May?"

"No," Elsa-May answered.

"Have a seat," Ettie said, looking at Kelly.

Once they were all seated, Ettie began, "Gossip says Sophie was at Titus's house the night he died."

Kelly raised his eyebrows and Ettie knew that was something he hadn't yet heard.

Elsa-May said, "Albie is selling his father's house to the next door neighbor, Billy Wilkes. He grew up Amish, but left a long time ago."

"Simon and Albie were arguing about Albie selling. It was an ugly scene. Simon wants to buy it and Albie won't sell it to him. Rumor is Simon won't pay the going rate, so his brother is selling to Billy."

"Wait a moment. Are you certain that Sophie was there with Titus the night he died?"

"Yes."

"That's not what she told me." He rubbed his forehead. "I'm going to sit on that information for a while and see if she trips herself up. Don't pass it on to anyone."

"We won't mention it," Elsa-May said, "but it's already going around the community."

Kelly cleared his throat. "I officially found out that Titus left everything to his son, Albie. One thing I haven't told you yet is the cause of death."

"What was it?" Ettie asked.

"Insulin. He died from an overdose of insulin."

"Would that have been painful?" Elsa-May asked.

"He would've gone into a hypoglycaemic coma and died from there. He would've been incoherent, with fuzzy thinking and slow speech before he slipped into the coma. Pretty much helpless."

"Would it have been a quick death?" Ettie inquired.

"No. I've been told it would've been quite slow, and for a while he'd have known what was happening. He didn't have seizures, but apparently that can happen, too."

Elsa-May shook her head. "It sounds like an awful way to go."

"No way is good, unless you die in your sleep. Well, I'm off home." He stood up. "Thanks for the information."

Ettie pushed herself to her feet. "This is an early night for you, isn't it?"

He nodded. "I'm making an effort. I've got a ton of paperwork back at the office. I'm waking at four tomorrow to get to the office to make a start. At least I'll be home today at a reasonable hour to keep the wife happy."

"That's important," Ettie said.

"Yes."

Both sisters walked him to the door. When he left, they closed the door and this time, they locked it.

"Did you really remember he was coming here, Elsa-May?"

"Of course I did. It had just temporarily left my mind. What about you?"

Ettie played along with Elsa-May's line of thinking. "I didn't forget. I just had a momentary memory lapse."

Elsa-May raised one eyebrow and stared at her. Ettie turned away and headed to let Snowy back inside, keeping her smile hidden from her sister.

CHAPTER 13

*E*arly the next morning Ettie and Elsa-May set off to Billy Wilkes's house, aiming to get there around eight in the morning.

"If he's not home we'll write a note on his door to tell him we stopped by."

Elsa-May nodded. "Okay."

As the taxi approached the house, the sisters saw people walking out the front door.

"That's Max and his wife, from the charity," Ettie said.

"*Jah*, it surely is," Elsa-May said after she squinted.

Ettie leaned forward and said to the driver. "Quick, let's stop and turn back."

The taxi driver hit the brakes.

"No, too late, they've already seen us."

"But they don't know it's us in the taxi, Elsa-May. They won't be able to see this far."

"What am I doing?" the driver asked raising his hands in the air. "Just tell me."

"Getting us out of here quickly," Ettie replied.

The driver wasted no time in doing a U-turn while the elderly sisters sank as low as they could in the back seat. Once they were back on the road, Ettie gave the driver Sophie's address that she'd gotten from someone at the funeral the day before.

"Why were they there?" Ettie asked Elsa-May. "How do they know Billy?"

"Something doesn't seem right."

"You know what else isn't right?" Ettie asked.

"What's that?"

"We can't show up at Sophie's house right now. It's far too early."

"Hm. We'll wait until her candle store opens and then go to her store. How's that?"

"Good idea, Elsa-May."

"Denke."

"Let's have a look around the markets while we're waiting."

"Okay."

Half an hour after Sophie's candle shop opened, Ettie and Elsa-May were sitting with her in the lunchroom of her candle store, sipping hot tea. She was the same old Sophie that she'd always been, kind and polite.

"I do miss everyone in the community. I know everyone was shocked that I left and they're probably all disappointed in me, but I just couldn't go on anymore. Titus wasn't the man he seemed. He showed a different side of himself to the boys and me, nothing like the front he put on for everyone else."

"What do you mean?" Ettie asked.

"I'm sorry to say he wasn't nice to us. He was grumpy, mean, and cranky. After the boys grew up and left, I couldn't take him anymore. I told him I'd rather die than stay with him for one more year. To everyone else, he was so calm and kind."

"I'm sorry to hear that," Elsa-May said.

"It wasn't only him, I guess. I mean, I couldn't blame him entirely for me leaving the community. Anyway, I plucked up the courage and left. Everything went fine for a few years, but then I realized how empty everything was. It no longer thrilled me that I was free to do anything anytime. It lost its attraction. I bought this store to keep me busy and keep my mind off things."

"Did you tell Titus how you felt?"

Sophie stared at Elsa-May. "Funny you should say that because we had recently started talking. Did you know that he gave me the money to buy the store?"

"*Nee*, we didn't."

She nodded. "He didn't want anyone to know. I don't think Albie even knows. Anyway, it was good of him. He had his good points. I won't say that he didn't. I told him I wouldn't take it at first—the money that was." Sophie sighed. "In the last few weeks, we had some long conversations about things. He wanted me to come back and he told me he'd changed."

"Were you rekindling your relationship?" Ettie asked her, wondering what she'd been doing there the night he'd been murdered and why she hadn't told Kelly. Could it have been she who killed Titus?

"I don't think rekindling is the right word for it. I don't think he could ever forgive me for leaving him alone for all those years, neither could I ever forget his treatment of me and the boys. He was making an effort to let me know he'd changed. I could've forgiven, but I never could've forgotten."

Ettie said, "He would've forgiven you if you had asked him to."

"I felt I didn't deserve another chance, and then how would I have known if he'd really changed? If I came back and he hadn't changed, I'd feel dreadful."

"Is that what you wanted?" Elsa-May asked. "To return?"

"I'm not sure. All I know is that he died too soon. I was enjoying our conversations. I had a glimpse of the man I'd once fallen in love with so long ago, then when I married him that man disappeared. How did I know the same thing wouldn't have happened again?"

"Did you visit him at the *haus?*" Elsa-May asked.

She nodded. "I visited him a couple of times."

"What about the day he died?" Ettie asked.

Sophie took a while to answer. "I saw him. I saw him dead and I didn't do anything about it. I didn't call the police or tell anyone. I didn't know what to do. He was already gone." She looked down into her tea. "I just left him there. I got into my car and drove away. I don't know why."

Ettie gasped. "Why didn't you call the police or paramedics when you saw that he'd been murdered?"

CHAPTER 14

Sophie continued talking to them about the night she found Titus dead in his house, "He didn't look like he'd been murdered. When the police talked to me, they said he had a syringe in him and he died of insulin overdose. But when I was there, he had no syringe anywhere near him."

"Have you thought about telling the police that?"

"No. I don't want them to think I did it. I don't want them to know I was there."

"Why would they think that?" Ettie asked.

"I'm not even sure."

"What was the problem, dear?" Elsa-May asked.

"The problem was me. I don't even know why I'm telling you this. I can't go through any questioning.

All I knew was I had nothing to do with it, and now he's gone. Nothing I do or say will bring him back."

"How did you know he was dead when you saw him?" Elsa-May asked.

"I knew he was gone. He wasn't breathing and there was no pulse."

"Did you see anything unusual around?"

"Like what?"

"I don't know, anything at all?"

Elsa-May and Ettie looked at each other trying to work things out.

"I went home and I couldn't sleep. I was sick several times. I think I was in shock. The police came in the morning and told me Max Burley found him, and then they told me about the syringe."

"I think you should tell them. They'd be most interested to know that when you saw him there was no syringe."

"I'd rather stay out of things. I can't handle death."

"The detective has to be told," Ettie said.

"Does he?"

Ettie nodded.

"I just hope they don't think I did it."

"Why would they think that?" Elsa-May asked.

"They've already asked me a ton of questions and I just don't want to go through any more. And, it would be dreadful if I turn around and admit to them that I lied to them."

"I know, but I think they'll overlook that when you deliver them that information about the syringe."

Right at that crucial moment, the bell on the door jingled, indicating a customer had walked through the door.

"I've got customers. Excuse me."

When Sophie stood up, Ettie said, "We won't keep you. We'll let you serve your customers."

"You don't have to go."

"We need to be on our way," Ettie said.

Elsa-May added, "We've got a full day ahead of us."

"Well, thank you both for stopping by. It's been so good to see you again."

"And you. We had no idea where you lived, but now we know."

"I don't leave the house much. Now that I've got the candle store, I still don't have far to go." Sophie gave a little laugh.

Ettie reached out and held Sophie's hand. "Please think about telling the police about what you saw."

"Do you think I should?"

"Yes, and the sooner, the better," Elsa-May said.

Ettie nodded agreeing with her sister since the

detective already knew. The longer she left telling him, the worse it would be.

"All right. I'll talk to the detective when I shut the store this afternoon."

Ettie patted her hand. "Good girl."

Ettie and Elsa-May headed out of the store and found a taxi.

Once they were in the back seat, Ettie said to her sister, "I hope Kelly doesn't come to see her. Maybe we should've told her we told the detective already because we heard the rumor from someone else."

"We'll just have to hope he doesn't. Now, what are we going to do about Billy?"

"Where to?" the driver asked.

"Just a minute," Ettie said as she turned to Elsa-May. "I don't know if we should go to Billy Wilkes's place now or ..."

"We'll give it a miss. If we go now, he'll probably figure out it was us in that taxi this morning and then he'll know we saw Max and his wife there. I'd feel stupid if he figured out it was us."

"Good point, we wouldn't want you to feel stupid."

"I'm turning the meter on," the driver said.

Ettie leaned forward and gave him their address. Then she turned to her sister. "Why don't we see what Max and his wife have got to say?"

"But we've only just seen them at the funeral. There would be nothing left to say to them. And they might put it together that we were the ones in the taxi this morning."

"Maybe Max and his wife were picking up a donation from Billy Wilkes."

"Maybe that's all it was."

"Do you think that Sophie and Titus were rekindling a romance?"

"According to Kelly she has a boyfriend, remember? If she wanted Titus back, she should've returned to the community first."

"Not everyone is as practical as you, Elsa-May. It sounded to me like Titus was the one who wanted her back. He even bought her the candle shop and I think that's because she could've kept the candle store when she returned to the community. I think Titus had a plan to win her back."

"Do you think someone knew that and didn't want her to come back?"

Ettie scratched her head under her *kapp* and then readjusted the pins holding her long gray hair in place. "I don't think that's it. I mean, who wouldn't have wanted her to come back?"

"A woman who wanted Titus for herself."

"But he couldn't marry again. Therefore, if your

theory is correct then she should've been killed to clear the way for the woman to marry him."

"Ettie, that's it. What if it was Sophie's male friend, the neighbor Kelly told us about? He can't have been happy about Sophie's husband buying her the candle store."

"You might be right, and if you are that means we wasted that visit. She didn't mention her neighbor and neither did we. Oh dear, there's so much to do. We have to find out what we can about the male friend of Sophie's and find out why the Burleys were at Billy's *haus*." Ettie sighed.

"We'll get there. We'll go home and have a rest and then we'll make a plan."

CHAPTER 15

*L*ater that afternoon, when Ettie was sitting stroking Snowy's soft fur, something jumped into her mind. She looked over at Elsa-May who was busily clicking her knitting needles together as she knitted a shawl.

"I just remembered something, Elsa-May. Something someone said about Titus."

Elsa-May looked over the top of her glasses at her.

"Someone said whatever was going on in Titus's life would come out in his crosswords."

"That's exactly what Albie told me at the funeral. Maybe not at the funeral, but I remember he told me that,"

"Jah, it was Albie who told me, too. Now, what if

the clue about the identity of his killer lay somewhere within one of his crosswords?"

"That's too far-fetched. Anyway, how would he have known who his killer was?" Elsa-May placed her knitting in her lap and stared at Ettie. "Think, Ettie. The only way he'd have known was if someone had threatened him."

"*Nee*, you're thinking too literally. I just want to get into Titus's head to see exactly what was going on in his life at the time. To do that, we need to see of all his recent crosswords." She fixed her beady eyes onto Elsa-May. "Now do you regret placing that crossword in the coffin?" She was still mad at her for doing that.

Elsa-May shook her head. "Now I see what this is about. You want to punish me for doing that. Just learn to let things go."

"I don't want to punish you! I still don't believe you actually did it, then again, that's an entirely different matter. Now, concentrate. What was on the crossword that you popped into the coffin?"

"I don't remember."

"Did you finish it?"

She nodded. "I finished it, but I never can remember them once I finish."

"You *have* to remember this time."

Elsa-May's face dropped.

"There's only one thing for it," Ettie said.

"What's that?"

"We'll have to dig up the body."

Elsa-May's knitting fell into her lap as her brows flew up towards her prayer *kapp*. "Ettie! Are you mad?"

"Very often, I am."

"We can't dig up the body. We can barely dig up a plant in our own garden. How are we going to move all that dirt from on top of the coffin? Anyway, I wouldn't agree to it."

"Well that's what we'll have to do unless you can tell me those words."

"Oh, botheration! Why can't you ever just let me relax and grow old in peace?"

"I will, after you tell me what those words were."

Elsa-May grunted. "I can't."

"You can and you must. I'll make you a cup of hot tea. If you relax, you'll recall the words." Ettie pushed herself to her feet. "Come on, Snowy, you can come with me." Snowy ran along behind Ettie and when they reached the kitchen, he sat on his dog bed in the corner of the room while watching her expectantly.

Snowy had three dog beds in the house, one in Elsa-May's bedroom, one in the corner of the living room near the fireplace, and one in the corner of the kitchen. He was accustomed to receiving a treat when he took his place in the kitchen, and Ettie obliged him. It kept him from being underfoot and begging when the sisters were cooking.

While Ettie made the tea, she wondered what else she could do to help Elsa-May relax. When she took the tea to Elsa-May, she placed it on the low table near her and then pulled up a chair. "Put your feet on the chair."

"Why?"

"It will help you to relax, and then you'll remember."

Elsa-May put her knitting in the bag by her feet, and then put her feet up on the chair.

"While you're drinking the tea, I'll sing a relaxing song." Ettie walked around the living room singing a hymn. Snowy followed her some of the way and then got bored when he realized Ettie wasn't going anywhere, and he stopped off and laid down on his living room bed.

"How is your atrocious singing relaxing me?" Elsa-May asked.

"Singing soothes and relaxes people. Everyone knows that."

"Not your singing. I don't mean to be rude, Ettie, but you've got a dreadful voice."

"You once told me I had a nice voice."

"That's probably when you were younger. It's changed."

"I've got the same voice I've always had."

"Nonsense! Voices change as a person ages."

"Nee they don't," Ettie said.

"Of course they do. Do you think you've got the same voice as a six-year-old child?"

"Nee, that's a bit extreme. But I've got the same sounding voice as I did when I was twenty."

"You don't, Ettie. Voices change all the time. People's voices mature and get croaky and quivery and deeper as they get older."

"Well, I'm sorry if my hymn was too croaky for you."

Elsa-May quietly sipped her tea.

Ettie glared at her, and then said, "If I annoy you so much I'll just go to the kitchen by myself." Sometimes Ettie just needed to get away from her annoying older sister. As soon as she sat down at the kitchen table, she heard Elsa-May screech.

"I remember!"

Ettie got back to her feet and hurried out of the kitchen, hoping Elsa-May was talking about the crossword and wasn't talking about something else she remembered. "What were they?"

"I remember that it was an old crossword that I

put into his coffin, and not the new one. It wouldn't have helped us."

This wasn't good. "Where's his new one—his latest one?"

"I throw them in the trash when I'm done. Why would I keep them?"

Ettie slumped onto the couch. "If that's so, why hadn't you thrown at that older one you put in the coffin?"

"I don't know."

Ettie sighed. "I really thought we had something there for a moment. I can't believe you threw it away"

"I'm sorry."

"Can you remember what any of the words were at least?"

"I already told you I never remember them once they're done. I don't store things in my head that aren't important. I can remember things like birthdays and things I need to remember, but a frivolous thing like a crossword is something I just don't store mentally."

"Very well," Ettie said in a small voice. "What we need to do is find, or somehow, get the crosswords that Kelly's evidence technicians took. Maybe those will help us."

"They're in evidence, Ettie, he's not going to hand them over just like that."

"We'll have to tell him our theory."

Slowly, Elsa-May nodded. "I suppose you're right this time, Ettie. We have no other choice."

CHAPTER 16

Kelly stared at them from the other side of his desk. "Do you mean to tell me that Titus knew beforehand who was going to kill him, and that he was going to be killed?"

Ettie gulped. This hadn't gone as well in person as it had played out in her head.

Elsa-May stared at Ettie. "Tell him, Ettie."

"No, we're not saying that, but we've got a pretty good idea that whatever was going on in his life he wrote a crossword about it. So there might be clues to his death hidden in his crosswords."

"Ettie doesn't think she's wasting your time about this," Elsa-May told him.

Kelly stared back and forth between the two of them. "Well, there might be something in what you're saying. It'll do no harm to take a look." He turned to his computer, tilted the screen toward him, and tapped on a few keys. "Let's see." After he pressed a few more buttons, the printer on the other side of his room made a whirring sound. He stood up and brought the pages back and passed some to Ettie and some to Elsa-May. "These are what we took from off his kitchen table."

"There's the word cheat, embezzlement…"

"And secret," Elsa-May added.

Ettie looked up at the detective. "Didn't you say that the owner of the charity was suspected of embezzlement?"

Kelly opened his mouth to answer her question and then his phone on his desk buzzed.

He picked up the receiver while Ettie read one of the other documents he'd handed them. She read the word 'love,' and similar terms of affection and then her attention was caught by Kelly's conversation.

"Hello … Are you certain?"

Ettie and Elsa-May looked at one another over Detective Kelly's shocked reaction.

And then Kelly said, "Let's go get him." He ended the call and then looked up at them. "We're going to have to cut this meeting short I'm afraid."

"Is this anything to do with Titus?"

"I can't say at this stage."

Ettie knew him well enough to know that was a 'yes.'

Elsa-May put her hands on the crosswords. "Can I take these with me?"

"No." He pulled them toward himself. "I'll stop by your place later when I can tell you more."

When they were outside the police station, Ettie said, "Elsa-May, did you hear what the caller said to Kelly?"

"Nee."

"I heard the whole thing. The caller said that it was Max's prints on the syringe."

"Prints on the syringe? He must've killed him."

"Ladies!"

They turned around to see Kelly hurrying to catch up to them.

"Did you visit Titus's wife like you said you were going to?"

Ettie looked at Elsa-May, and then said, "I'm certain she's going to come and tell you herself; she said she would."

"Mrs. Smith, I don't have a lot of time. Tell me what?"

"When Sophie was there the night he died, there was no syringe in sight."

"What?" he yelled.

Ettie cringed.

"He was dead when she was there? She found him? Is that true?" he asked.

Slowly, Ettie nodded. "That's what Sophie told us."

He sighed heavily. "This is something you should've told me right away. He told us he didn't touch the syringe, he said he didn't touch anything. He's guilty by his own admission. We had him, and now you ruin things by telling me that she found him prior with no syringe?"

Elsa-May tugged Ettie's sleeve. "Come on, Ettie, we should go."

"Thanks for the help, ladies, but you leave me in a quandary." He stomped away.

"What was all that about?" Elsa-May asked.

"He was going to arrest Max, but now he can't. Not if Sophie already saw him dead before Max got there. Then there's the matter of the conflicting stories over the syringe, and the fingerprints. You see?"

"I think so."

"He was just about to arrest Max because the caller just now said that Max's prints were on the syringe. Our information about Sophie meant that he was already dead and it's possible the syringe had nothing to do with it."

"It must've Ettie, because he was killed with the insulation."

"Insulin, Elsa-May." Ettie sighed. "Don't worry."

"I'm not worried, I'm just saying—"

"It's all about the timing of the thing."

Elsa-May gave a nod. "Why didn't you just say that?"

"I thought I did."

Ettie and Elsa-May walked up the road.

"Well that's it, then," Elsa-May said.

"What's it?"

"Max embezzled from the charity, Titus found out and wasn't happy about it. Maybe Titus gave him an ultimatum to pay all the money back and when he didn't, Titus was going to blow the whistle."

Ettie grimaced. "Don't say 'blow the whistle.'"

"Why not?"

"Just say he was going to expose him for being a fraud."

"I prefer to say 'blow the whistle.' It's quicker and snappier. Anyway, that's it."

"Do you think so?" Ettie asked.

"Jah. He killed Titus to cover up his taking the money out of the charity. Titus would've been furious that the money wasn't going to the right people. He put a lot of work into that charity."

"Maybe Max was framed, or someone is trying to frame him."

"Stop looking for problems where they don't exist, Ettie. No one's framing him."

Ettie sighed. "It just seems too easy that it's Max. And why would he call the police and say he found the body if he was one who killed him?"

"He had a reason. If he found the body, he wouldn't appear guilty. Don't you get it? I think that's quite clever. Maybe the police never suspect the person who finds the body."

Ettie hunched her shoulders. "I don't think you're right. I'd say the opposite would be true."

"Forget it, Ettie. The riddle has been solved, the last letter has been placed on the crossword. It's over."

Ettie shook her head as they stood still on the sidewalk. "It doesn't quite fit. The pieces don't go together, or I should say, the letters don't fit the boxes, but I hope you're right"

"I always am. I think that Sophie didn't notice the syringe, but it was there all along. She was so distraught to find her beloved dead that she just didn't see it."

"Beloved? She told us she didn't feel that way about him."

"She might have when she found him dead," Elsa-May said.

Ettie looked up the street. "I've got a good idea, why don't we—"

"Go up to the road to that nice little café and—"

"Have a slice of cake?"

Elsa-May chuckled. "Good idea, I'm glad I—"

"Thought of it?"

Elsa-May smiled and linked her arm through Ettie's. "All's well that ends well, Ettie."

Ettie pushed her lips into a pout.

"Aw, are you upset because the detective figured out who did it before you did?"

"Don't be silly, Elsa-May. That's his job to do that. We were just helping him, that's all. Anyway, nothing's figured out. There are just more questions."

"How ironic. Titus would've loved to have all this intrigue—all these questions and puzzles to be answered. He would've also been tickled pink that his crosswords might have figured in his death."

Ettie wasn't listening to Elsa-May's prattles as they walked up the road. She was too busy trying to put the whole thing out of her mind. Maybe Max had been stealing money from the charity for years and maybe Titus had found out. But wouldn't sparking a murder investigation increase the risk of the money scam being exposed?

"You're thinking again, Ettie."

"It's quite hard not to think about Titus and what really happened."

Elsa-May sighed. "Okay, tell me what you're thinking."

Ettie told her sister what had been on her mind.

"Max might not have thought the whole thing through," countered Elsa-May. "He might have killed Titus in a panic and hadn't thought of the ramifications of a murder investigation. But I understand what you mean because he was already under investigation for fraud, and someone who worked a lot for the charity being murdered —*jah*, I see what you mean. It doesn't make sense. Should we tell Detective Kelly?"

"*Nee*, of course not. What do we know? Well, one thing I know is that the murder had to have been planned. He wasn't killed spontaneously with something nearby. Someone had to have brought the insulin with them. It's common sense."

"I agree, it was obviously planned."

Ettie shrugged. "All I know is I'm just going to keep out of the whole thing for a while."

"Good idea." They arrived at the café, and Elsa-May put her hand on the door handle. "Here we are. Now we can think about something important—our cake selections."

Ettie chuckled.

Elsa-May pushed open the door, and allowed Ettie through first.

The café had the best cake selection in town and it was just a short walk from the police station. Ettie chose a strawberry shortcake, while Elsa-May opted for the orange and poppy seed cake with the thick icing. As they usually did, ever since they figured out the wisdom of each making a separate selection, they shared.

CHAPTER 17

Once they were back in their own home, Ettie got to thinking again. "Maybe we should visit Sophie again."

"You said you weren't going to do anything or even think about it anymore."

"I'm not thinking about Titus, I'm thinking about Sophie."

"Same difference."

Ettie pushed her lips out. "Will I have to go by myself?"

Elsa-May sighed. *"Nee,* I'll go with you. Are we doing it today or tomorrow?"

"Let's do it now."

"We've already been out today."

"Do I have to go alone?"

"Nee, I'll come." Another sigh followed.

. . .

When Elsa-May and Ettie arrived at Sophie's store with a bag of cookies, they were surprised. She had a man with her. He was introduced as Tyson Jones. And they learned that he lived next door to her. This was the man Kelly had told them about.

"Tyson was just hanging some lights for me," Sophie said.

"That's very kind of you," Elsa-May said to him.

He gave her a smile. "I don't mind, it's not a hard thing for me to do."

"Will you stay for some hot tea, or coffee?" Sophie asked them.

"We'd love to," Ettie said.

"We're not keeping you from your work, are we?"

"It's okay, it's usually quiet at this time of day."

"And what about you, Tyson?" Sophie asked.

"I wouldn't mind a cup of hot tea. As long as I'm not intruding."

"Don't mind us," Elsa-May said.

Ettie was pleased to have a chance to question this man because she had heard two reports. One that Sophie was trying to rekindle a romance with Titus, and the other that she was having a relationship with Tyson. The next few minutes might determine which one of those was true.

THE LAST WORD

As he continued to fiddle with the light, Ettie asked, "Have you lived in the area for a long time, Tyson?"

"I was raised here, in the house right next door to Sophie's. I moved away, but when my parents passed away I moved back into the house. That was about the same time that Sophie moved in."

Sophie smiled. "It's nice to have good neighbors like we have here. I tell them all the time that I appreciate them."

He chuckled. "We're all like this in the street here. We help each other out and look out for one another. If there's anyone visiting in the street or someone we don't know, we keep an eye out and make sure they're supposed to be there."

"I imagine being so close to the markets that there'd be people coming and going quite often."

"I meant at night, sorry, at unusual times, when the market's not open."

"It's a shame Titus didn't have the same set-up in his street," Ettie said.

"Oh, yes, your ex-husband," Tyson said as he looked over at Sophie.

"Well, it's a bit hard when each home is built on over forty acres. You can't see who's coming and going at your neighbor's house," Sophie said as she placed down a tray of four tea cups and the cookies on a plate.

"I suppose that's true." He climbed down the ladder. "I should go and get some work done at home and I'll leave you ladies to your chatting."

"What about your hot tea, Tyson." Ettie's eyes flicked to his cup.

"I remembered I have an important job to do."

"Take one of our cookies with you," Ettie said.

"Or two," Elsa-May added as she offered him the plate.

"No, thank you. They look great, but I'm a diabetic," he said with a smile.

Elsa-May lowered the plate to the table and Ettie made a mental note. She was glad when Elsa-May didn't react to what he said. She knew Elsa-May would've concluded that Sophie had access to his insulin since she was a close friend. She could've easily gone to his house and taken a syringe and some insulin without him missing it. She had already admitted being at Titus's house that night, so she was there around the time he died and she had access to her friend's insulin. Or, were Sophie and Tyson in it together?

After they said goodbye to Tyson, Sophie walked him out. Ettie stared at Sophie's back wondering if she'd killed her estranged husband and if so, what had been her motive? That was something they needed to find out. The more Ettie thought about it, the more she thought Tyson didn't do it. If he had, he wouldn't have mentioned so freely that he was a diabetic.

And what about Max's fingerprints being found on the syringe? Were they—Max and Sophie—perhaps in it together? And where might that strange partnership have come from?

When Sophie returned, they had a quick cup of tea with her while keeping the conversation light, and then they left.

CHAPTER 18

The next day, Elsa-May and Ettie were still trying to figure things out.

"I didn't talk to Simon at the funeral."

Elsa-May shook her head. "Neither did I."

"Maybe he knows something."

"Do you think he killed his *vadder?*"

"Nee, but I think we should talk with him, don't you?"

"I suppose so, but do you know where he lives?"

"Nee, but I'm pretty sure I know who does."

Fifteen minutes later, they arrived at Aunt Agnes's house.

"Here you both are. Come in and sit down. It'll only take me five minutes to get ready."

"Ready for what?" Ettie asked her.

"To visit Sophie." She looked at Ettie and Elsa-May's blank faces. "Isn't that why you're here?"

"Nee, it's not," Elsa-May said flatly.

Aunt Agnes lips turned down at the corners. "Don't you remember at the funeral you said you were going to visit Sophie and I said stop by and fetch me? If you haven't come here for that, then why?"

"We came to ask you where Simon lives."

"Are you going to visit Simon now?"

"If we can find out where he lives we will."

A smile brightened her crinkly face. "I can take you there in the buggy."

"That would be good, *denke."*

"It'll take me five minutes to change into a going-out dress."

Ettie slumped into the couch while Aunt Agnes hurried out of the room.

"You should've known this would happen, Ettie." Elsa-May sat down beside her.

"Why would she want to come with us?"

"I don't know. Perhaps she's just lonely."

A few minutes later, Aunt Agnes breezed out of her bedroom in clothes that didn't look much different.

"How do I look? This is a new dress. I just finished it last week."

"Wunderbaar!" Ettie said. "Are you ready?"

"I need to hitch the buggy, and you can help."

Ettie and Elsa-May helped to hitch the buggy and then they were ready to go.

"Would he be at work at this time of day?" Elsa-May asked Agnes.

"He works from home. He's an accountant."

"Oh, I didn't know that," Ettie said.

"The thing with me is that I listen when people talk to me."

"That's good," Elsa-May said. "More people should keep their ears open."

"Funny you should say that, Elsa-May, considering the problem with your hearing the other day."

Elsa-May chuckled and told Aunt Agnes about her ear blockages causing Ettie some grief.

"I can sympathize with you there, Ettie. I had an old aunt who was deaf, and instead of saying, 'I beg your pardon,' she always guessed what I was saying, and it was always wrong. It led to quite some frustration. Anyway, that aside, I happen to know that Simon is unmarried, but has two children out of wedlock but they don't live with him." She made tsk tsk sounds with her tongue. "It's a shame really."

"We had no idea," Elsa-May said.

"It's the kind of thing that Titus wouldn't want too many people to know. He wasn't happy that his youngest son left the community and led such a complicated life. That's what happens when people leave us."

"Two of my *dochders* are still out of the community," Ettie said. "I pray every day for them."

"All we can do is pray they come back, Ettie."

"Have you ever been to his house before, Agnes?"

"I have. I drove someone there once for tax advice. Now that's just jogged my memory. It was Simon who introduced his *vadder* to the founders of the homeless people's charity."

"Simon introduced Titus to Max and Terese?"

"Teresa," Agnes corrected Elsa-May. "And, *jah*, that's right."

Elsa-May looked at Agnes. "Terese is how she introduced herself to me at the funeral. I'm going to assume that's right."

When they stopped the buggy outside of Simon's house, he opened the door and stuck his head out. When they looked at him, he waved to them and stepped outside, closing the door behind him. With his hands in his pockets, he slowly sauntered toward them.

"Hello, ladies."

Ettie was the first to step down from the buggy.

"Hello, Simon."

When they had all exchanged greetings, there was silence between the four of them.

Since it didn't seem like he was going to invite them inside, Ettie asked, "Simon, I have a question."

"Sure."

"What do you know about Max Burley and his wife, Terese?"

"I know they aren't exactly aboveboard. My guess is they're skimming money off that charity they set up."

"But didn't you introduce them to your *vadder?*" Aunt Agnes asked.

"That was many years ago. They used to be clients of mine before I cut them off. They wanted me to do certain things that I wasn't willing to do. They've got a bad name now. I've heard some things."

"Is that what you told your *vadder?*" Elsa-May asked.

He scoffed. "I told him, but he wouldn't have a bar of it."

"Who do you think killed your *vadder?*" Ettie asked.

His eyes bugged open at the unexpected question. "Oh. Well." He blinked a couple times. "Most likely Harold."

"Harold?" Elsa-May asked.

Ettie recalled that Titus had a half-brother. "He wasn't at the funeral, was he? I didn't see him if he was."

"He wasn't at the funeral, you're right about that," he said. "He was cut out of an inheritance too, just like me. Just because I left the community, I was cut off with not even one cent from the old man."

"He was never even mentioned at the funeral," Aunt Agnes said, referring to Harold.

Simon shook his head. "I haven't seen him for ages."

"He left the community a long time ago, didn't he?" Elsa-May asked.

"That's right."

"Why would he have killed him after all these years?"

"What Elsa-May means is do you know the last time your *vadder* saw him?"

"Harold stopped by and visited him every now and again."

"Why would he do that if he and your *vadder* didn't get along?"

He shrugged. "Probably just to have another argument."

"Was he a diabetic?" Elsa-May asked.

Simon was visibly shocked at the question and Ettie saw that he swallowed hard.

"Why do you ask?" Simon said.

"Because of the way your *vadder* was killed."

"I'm a diabetic, but I didn't kill him."

"You're diabetic?" Ettie asked.

"That's right. I wasn't born that way. It's a product of a bad diet and no exercise, I'm afraid. Anyway, if you'll excuse me, I've got a client coming in a minute. Otherwise, I would've invited you all in."

"That's fine," Ettie said. "We probably should've called before we stopped by."

"It was nice to see you all again."

They said goodbye and headed off in Aunt Agnes's buggy.

CHAPTER 19

While the horse trotted down the road, Ettie sat back and closed her eyes while letting all the information percolate through her head.

"Let me help you both," Aunt Agnes said, jolting Ettie to the core.

"Help us to do what?" Elsa-May asked.

"I know what you are trying to do. You're helping that detective who is trying to find out who killed Titus. I can be of help. I'll tell you what I know. Sophie was there the night Titus died. She was at his house. Max, the crooked charity man, found him in the morning and then there was a syringe sticking out of his neck, and he was killed with insulin."

Elsa-May said, "Sophie said she didn't see a syringe sticking out of his neck."

"Ah, then, now I know she admitted to you that she was there the night he died, and was the one who found him and not Max."

Ettie glared at Elsa-May for letting that slip. Aunt Agnes had set a trap and Elsa-May had fallen into it.

Agnes turned around and looked at Elsa-May in the back seat. "And that means you went there without me."

"We just saw her briefly when we were in town," Ettie said.

"Anyway," Elsa-May said, "Now we know that Max isn't putting the money where he should. Good thing the authorities are onto him. He won't get away with it."

"Who do you think killed Titus, Ettie?" Agnes asked.

"I don't know."

"I'll miss him. He always gave me every single crossword. I think I have every single one he ever did."

Ettie lunged forward and sat on the edge of her seat. "Do you still have them?"

"Jah."

"Can we see them?"

"Why?"

"Because there might be a clue amongst them."

"A clue to who killed him?"

THE LAST WORD

"We think so," Elsa-May said.

"Okay. I have them all in a box. I was taking you back to your *haus,* but if I take this next road to the left, then we'll get to mine in no time."

Soon they were sitting in Aunt Agnes's living room.

"This is the last one he gave me," Agnes said pulling a piece of paper out of the box.

Elsa-May stared at it. "That's the same one he gave me."

"The same as the one you had on the day of the funeral?" Ettie asked.

"Jah."

"So, it wasn't an older one you had like you thought, it was a recent one?"

"Jah, I guess that's so."

Ettie sighed exasperated by her sister's confusion.

They stared at the crossword for so long that Aunt Agnes said, "Keep it if you want."

"Are you sure?" Ettie asked.

"Of course. Would you like me to take you home now, or would you like me to fix you some lunch?"

Ettie and Elsa-May looked at each other.

"We might just get a taxi home," Ettie said.

"Nonsense, I can drive you. I didn't unhitch the buggy yet."

"Elsa-May's still not feeling too well and a taxi will get us home much quicker."

"Very well, I'll call for taxi from the barn for you."

"Denke, Agnes."

"Why don't you take the whole box of crosswords and bring them back once you're done with them?"

"Could we?" Elsa-May asked.

"Jah."

A few minutes later, Ettie and Elsa-May were outside Agnes's house waiting for the taxi while Agnes unhitched her horse and buggy.

"We must go to Detective Kelly."

"What is it, Ettie?"

"I've got a good idea who killed Titus."

"What about Harold?"

"What about him?"

"Whatever your brilliant conclusion is, shelve it. At least until we find out about Harold."

Ettie pursed her lips. "Okay, how do we do that? How do we find out where he is?"

"Who knows everyone's business?"

Ettie pointed to herself. "Me?"

"Nee! Aunt Agnes."

"Quick, go back and ask her where he might be."

Elsa-May grunted. "We should've done that when he was first mentioned."

"You go, and I'll wait in case the taxi comes."

Elsa-May hurried back to talk to Agnes. When the taxi arrived, Elsa-May was still talking to Agnes. Ettie got into the taxi first and then a minute later, Elsa-May joined her in the back seat.

"Where to?" the driver asked.

Elsa-May gave an address that Ettie recognized as being close to the town center.

As the taxi drove away, Ettie said, "Are we going to see Harold?"

"Jah."

"He still lives locally?"

"According to the local gossip, he does."

"What does he do with himself?"

"He runs a small key-cutting kiosk. And that's where we're going—downtown."

"I didn't know we had a downtown."

"Every town has a 'downtown.'"

Ettie scratched her nose and wondered if she'd recognize Harold. It had been so long since she'd seen him."

CHAPTER 20

*E*ttie squirmed in the back seat to make herself comfortable as she tried to recall images of Harold. Harold and Titus had the same mother. Harold's father died when Harold was quite young and several years later his mother remarried, and then they had Titus. She could picture Harold at his mother's wedding, and he seemed in her mind to be a child of six or seven.

"What are you going to say to him, Ettie?" Elsa-May asked.

Ettie opened her eyes and looked at her. "Me? What am I going to say?"

Elsa-May nodded. *"Jah."*

"Why is it always me who has to come up with everything?"

"Because I ran back and asked Aunt Agnes where we could find him."

Ettie had thought it strange that Elsa-May had gone back to see Agnes without complaining. "I didn't see much running going on."

"You know what I mean."

"We could just ask him how he is, and then talk about Titus."

"And just see what he says?" asked Elsa-May.

"Exactly. I don't think there's anything else we can do."

When the taxi let them out, they walked through the small suburban mall until they came to a locksmith's kiosk in the center.

Elsa-May dug Ettie in the ribs. "There he is, over there."

As soon as Ettie took another step, she saw him. He was tucking into a large sandwich. He had aged considerably, and gray hair was sticking out from both sides of his head while the top of his head was bald.

"He's put on a lot of weight."

"You think everybody's fat, Ettie."

When he looked up, he smiled at them. He seemed to be pleased to see them. He swallowed what was in his mouth, stood up and dabbed at his mouth with a paper napkin.

"It's nice to see the two of you. How have you both been?"

"We've been well," Elsa-May said.

"What brings you to this neck of the woods?"

"We missed you at Titus's funeral. We expected you to be there, so we thought we'd come and say hi."

"That's very kind of you. I thought about going, but then I thought better of it. I said farewell to him in my own way."

"Did you ever make amends with him?" Ettie asked.

"No! He never apologized."

"For what?" Elsa-May asked.

"It doesn't matter. I wouldn't know where to start. He cheated me out of my inheritance. Now I hear he's caused the same to happen to one of his own sons."

"One inherited, the other didn't," Ettie said.

He sat down again. "Excuse me if I keep eating. I have to eat when I can get a break." He took another bite of his sandwich. It was a large take-out sandwich, going by the wrapping, full of greasy meat dripping with fat. It turned Ettie's stomach to look at it. When he finished chewing the food in his mouth, he continued, "Like I said to the cops, I didn't know him well enough to know who might've had it in for him." He looked down at the sandwich. "It's no secret I never liked him."

Ettie and Elsa-May looked at one another.

"But I didn't kill him." He looked up at them again. "Is that why you're here? Hoping for a full confession?"

The ladies giggled.

"Of course not," Ettie said.

"As we said, we just missed you at the funeral," Elsa-May added.

"I bet no one else did. Excuse me." He went to the other end of the kiosk to serve someone. It was a lady who wanted a key cut and said she'd be back in half an hour.

While he was talking with his customer, Ettie looked over and saw a newspaper with a half-finished crossword puzzle. When he came back, she said, "Your brother liked crosswords as well."

"I think that's the only thing we had in common, apart from our mother."

Elsa-May said, "He constructed them, you know. He gave me the last one he did before he died and it was very interesting and informative."

Elsa-May stared at him with raised eyebrows.

He stared into her face. "What do you mean?"

"It's well known amongst Titus's friends that whatever was going on in his life at the time, he recorded it in his crosswords. The police have a theory about it, but they weren't able to get the last crossword, but now I've just found it."

"Is that so?"

Elsa-May nodded.

"Do you mind if I take a look at it for old time's sake?"

"I don't have it with me," Elsa-May said.

"Can I stop by your house after I finish work?"

"Okay."

"Do you still live in that big house down by the old mill?"

"I haven't lived there for years. Ettie and I moved in together after our husbands died. If you give me a piece of paper, I'll write down the address for you."

He gave Elsa-May a pen and paper, and Ettie stood there watching Elsa-May write down their address while wondering what her sister was thinking. Harold unnerved her, how keen he was to see that crossword.

When they had said goodbye and walked away, Ettie said, "Good one, Elsa-May. Now we've got him coming to the house and he could very well be the killer. Did you see how interested he was to get his hands on that crossword after what you said about it?"

"I did. Do you think we should tell Kelly?" Elsa-May asked.

"Maybe, but tell him what exactly?"

"Well, do you think he's the killer, Ettie?"

"I didn't think he was until he wanted that crossword so badly. Particularly after what you just said." As they walked up the street keeping their eyes open for a taxi, Ettie said. "Let's go over what we've found out lately. We've found two diabetics. Sophie's neighbor, and Simon."

"And Harold still hates his brother," added Elsa-May.

"You shouldn't have made such a big deal out of that crossword."

Elsa-May shrugged. "I just wanted to draw him out a bit. I didn't want him to come to the house, but what could I do?"

Ettie bit her lip. "I know."

"That was silly of me to give him our address. How would I know that would happen? He can't kill the both of us."

Ettie nodded. "That's true."

"You think you know something, Ettie?"

"Hmm. Now I'm thinking it might be a good idea he's coming to the house. We can find out what he knows about the charity founders, Max and Terese."

"If he knows anything at all. I wonder if Kelly made that arrest. I think he's angry with us now and I think we should give him some time to cool down," Elsa-May said.

"If he's suspicious of Harold and he knows Harold's coming to our house, he'd certainly warn us," Ettie said. "That's why I think we should tell him."

"Good idea. I would feel much better about Harold coming to the house if Kelly knows he's coming there. Although he seemed harmless enough."

"Except when the crossword was mentioned," Ettie reminded her.

"If he killed him, he would've seen the crosswords on the table."

"Yes, but he wouldn't have known their significance." On their way to the station, Ettie came up with a better idea. "We're going to go to Billy Wilkes's house soon, but before that, we'll invite people to our *haus* tonight for a get-together."

"Who?"

"Everyone. Albie, Simon, their mother, Sophie, her diabetic neighbor, and then, of course, Harold, who's coming anyway. We'll also invite Max and Terese and they'll be pleased to be invited because they're looking for another Amish person to take over from Titus. And probably Billy, too. Is that all of them?"

"I think so."

CHAPTER 21

They arrived at Billy Wilkes's house after they'd invited the rest of the guests for the coming evening.

Billy was driving away from the house and the taxi met the car. Ettie and Elsa-May flagged him down. He stopped the car and got out.

Dipping his head down, he looked into the taxi. "Hello."

Ettie got out. "Hello. We were just coming to see how you are."

"Mrs. Smith?"

"Jah. It's Mrs. Smith. I'm glad you remember me. I'm here with my sister, Elsa-May Lutz. We just want to talk to you about Titus Graber."

He looked into the taxi and saw Elsa-May. "Come on up to the house."

"Are you sure?"

"Yes"

"Weren't you going somewhere?"

"That can wait."

Ettie got back in, and the taxi drove her and Elsa-May the rest of the distance to the house. They paid the driver, got out and joined Billy who was now on the porch.

"Come in." As they walked inside, he said, "I'm trying to think of the last time I saw the both of you. It must've been years ago."

The last time they'd seen *him* was when he'd been talking with the crooked charity people, but Ettie kept quiet about that. He showed them into his living room. Ettie recognized the furniture and the brightly colored rug on the floor as being expensive. He was doing well for himself. She sat on the couch, and it was so comfortable she never wanted to get up.

"What is it you want to tell me? I suppose you've heard that Titus's son is selling me his land?"

"We heard that."

"Is the community upset about that, or something?"

Elsa-May chuckled. "Not at all."

He drew his eyebrows together in confusion.

While Ettie tried to figure out whether the huge

rug covering most of the floor was one of those expensive Persian carpets, she heard Elsa-May talking.

"We're wondering if you know anything about a couple called Max and Terese Burley. Titus was quite close with them."

Ettie whipped her head up to look at Billy, pleased with what Elsa-May had said.

"Yes, I met them recently. They visited me just a couple of days ago."

"What did they want?"

"They asked me about making a donation. I get a ton of requests, usually by email, or direct mail. It was quite surprising to have people turn up on my doorstep like that. Then Max told me he was close with Titus, and Titus did work for him."

Ettie wondered if he knew them better than what he was saying. "That's the first and only time you met them?"

"Yes. I've never seen them before in my life. Why?"

"We just heard some talk, that's all."

"About me?"

"Nee," Elsa-May said, "About the Burleys. It might not be true. Do you know that Max Burley was the one to find Titus?"

Billy nodded. "He told me that. Poor old Titus."

"You got along with him?"

He laughed. "Never. We never saw eye-to-eye about anything. I'm only happy that Albie saw some sense and agreed to sell to me."

Ettie wondered if that was a good enough motive to kill a man, to get his next of kin to sell him the property. Probably not. Especially since it looked like Billy had plenty of money and could afford to do without the added land.

Elsa-May stood and looked out his large picture window. "From here, you get a good view of Titus's house."

Billy jumped up, walked over to where she was, and looked out the window. "A good view. If I had some binoculars."

"It's a distance away, I admit, but you'd be able to see cars that came and went."

"Yes. That's true."

"Did you happen to see any cars lately? Maybe the same car frequently?"

Ettie recalled she had seen a fairly new-looking turquoise blue car parked in the driveway of Sophie's house. "A bright blue one perhaps?"

"Yes, I possibly noticed a blue one, but I couldn't swear to it. I don't sit here looking out the window all day." He chuckled. "Anyway, I must keep moving. Can I drive you ladies anywhere?"

"Are you heading into town?"

"Close to town. I can take you there, it's not much out of the way."

"Thank you," Elsa-May said. "We'd like to be dropped at the police station."

His face went white. "Police station?"

"Yes, we need to tell the detective something."

"About me?"

"No," Ettie said. "Something else."

"I had a detective come by asking me all kinds of questions. I never got along with Titus, and, yes I wanted his land—always have, but I didn't kill him. He made me so angry leaving his land the way he had. Leaving it bare, doing nothing. He could've at least let me lease it if he didn't want to sell, but he just wouldn't. He was a cranky, spiteful old goat of a man."

Elsa-May looked at him in shock. Ettie was forming a clearer picture of the other side of Titus's personality, the side of him that his family members talked about. They'd said he showed one side to the community, which was the nice side that she'd seen, but then he'd had his darker side.

"I'm sorry, I shouldn't talk like that. I'll drive you to the police station. Just don't tell them I saw a blue car. I'm not totally sure about it."

Ettie nodded. They already knew that Sophie had

visited Titus, so it didn't really matter whether he'd seen her car or not.

Just before Ettie got out of Billy's car, she said, "I have a few people coming to our house tonight, and Elsa-May and I would love it if you'd be there."

"Amish?"

"And some *Englischers*." Knowing he'd want to keep in good with Albie until he officially owned Titus's land, Ettie said, "Albie will be there."

"Oh, will he?"

Ettie smiled and nodded.

"What time?"

"Seven."

"Sure, I'm not doing anything else. I'll be there."

CHAPTER 22

Once all their guests were seated, some on extra chairs they had to bring in from the kitchen, Ettie stood up and said, "Who killed Titus?"

"Do you expect one of us to know?" Simon asked.

"You don't think one of us did it, do you?" Max Burley asked.

Ettie turned her attention to Max. "Might I start with you, Max?"

"What do you mean?"

"It's not a secret that ... well, there are rumors that you weren't aboveboard in your financial dealings with the charity."

He bounded to his feet. "Now wait a minute."

His wife tugged on his sleeve. "Don't be stupid. Sit down."

Max sat down but not before he glared at Simon, who looked away from him.

Ettie stared at Simon. "Now, Simon."

"Yes?" He stared back at Ettie.

"You didn't get along with your father."

"I tried, but he wasn't an easy man to get along with. I didn't kill him."

"No, I don't believe you did." Ettie's gaze traveled around the room and rested on Terese. "Terese, you were also involved in the charity and I believe both you and your husband are the founders."

"Yes, but if you're trying to say we did anything wrong, we didn't. We've heard the rumors and we've got all our paperwork in order. Are you trying to imply we killed Titus to cover up some imaginary illegal dealings?"

"I didn't say that at all, but it's interesting that you did. Now, we also have Albie."

"Jah?" Albie said.

"You are the sole heir of your father's estate. You are the one with the most to gain."

"I didn't kill him." Albie's voice was quiet, almost a whisper.

"Why am I here?" a voice from behind Ettie rang out.

Ettie swung around to face Harold. "You're here because you hated your brother."

"I did, but I didn't give him two thoughts for years. He was already out of my life, so I didn't need to kill him."

"This is ridiculous," Sophie said standing up. "We're leaving."

"No, Sophie," Elsa-May said. "I don't think that would be a good idea."

"Why's that?"

"Sit down for a moment, Sophie," Ettie said. "This is what happened the night that Titus Graber died. If there was one thing Titus loved it was a challenge. That's why he loved his crosswords, and the other great love of his life was you, Sophie."

Sophie looked down and her friend, Tyson, looked surprised.

Ettie continued, addressing everyone, "Titus set himself a challenge and that was to win Sophie back. He developed different reasons to talk with her and to lure her to his house. He bought her a candle store to make her feel softer toward him. He called you that night, didn't he, Sophie? The night he died."

She nodded. "Yes, he did."

"Did he arrange an exact time for you to get there?"

"Yes, and he was most insistent that I shouldn't be late."

Ettie looked over at Billy. "Billy—"

"It's Bill."

"Sorry. Bill, you saw Sophie go to the house that night, didn't you? You've got a clear view from your house. I believe you kept an eye on the man who wouldn't sell to you because you were desperate for his land."

"I wouldn't say desperate, but you're right, I saw her that night. I didn't want to get involved and testify about anything. How did you know?"

"Gossip got around and it had to have started from somewhere. I think I'm right in concluding that no one in this room killed Titus."

Albie said, "What are you talking about, Ettie?"

"He gave himself a shot of insulin that he took from Simon's house." She looked over at Simon. "I'm guessing he visited you in the last couple of weeks?"

Simon nodded. "It's true. He was acting odd."

Ettie continued, "Hmm. I figured out what happened. It was something that Elsa-May said, and then everything clicked."

"What did I say?" Elsa-May asked.

"You said Titus liked a challenge and you also said that Sophie might have changed the way she thought about him when she saw him dead. That got me to thinking. Titus gave himself a shot of insulin to make himself ill, hoping when Sophie saw him so ill, she'd realize she loved him and didn't want to lose him. Then his plan was he'd equalize his blood sugar with all that candy he had in the kitchen, eating it when Sophie wasn't looking."

Sophie said, "But what about the syringe in his neck? When I was there I didn't see anything."

"Ah, that's because it wasn't there. He injected himself then placed the syringe out of sight."

"That's right, Mrs. Smith." Max said, "No one killed him. Titus told me what he was planning to do. I begged him not to do it. He said he wouldn't when he saw how strongly I disapproved. I woke up with a bad feeling in my gut and I drove to his house and found him dead. I panicked and found the syringe and then jabbed it in his neck to make it look like a murder, not a suicide. I knew that's what it'd look like. I didn't want Titus's family to know about his stupid idea, and neither did I want them to think that he suicided."

"Why didn't you tell the police?" Elsa-May asked.

"Like I said, I didn't want the family to know."

Kelly stepped out of one of the back bedrooms. "Is that right, Mr. Burley?" He looked from Max to Sophie.

"That's what happened," Max said.

Sophie remained silent while a single tear trickled down her face. "Why wouldn't he have just pretended to be sick?"

Max said, "I suggested that, and he said he'd never been good at lying and he wouldn't be convincing."

Albie moved closer and put his arm around his mother.

"All the evidence confirms what Mrs. Smith has just explained. Would anyone else like to add anything?"

"He put himself in danger over you, Sophie," Harold said.

She looked at Harold and nodded. "I never wanted that to happen."

"No, but it's convenient. You don't have to pay back the money he loaned you for your store." Harold spat out his words. "His money was the same money I was cheated out of."

"He gave me that money," Sophie said.

"No, he didn't," Simon said. "He talked to me about it. I knew the old snake was never going to leave me anything, or you, Mother, if you didn't go back with him. He told me the deal he made with you. You were to pay him back at three hundred dollars a week. He said you told him you'd easily be able to pay him back through the candle sales and the rent coming in from the adjoining shop, which was on the same title."

Everyone looked at Sophie.

THE LAST WORD

Ettie stared at her. "Sophie, you knew the symptoms he had. I believe he was still alive when you got there."

Sophie shook her head. "Ettie, that's not what you just said."

Ettie continued, "You'd seen the symptoms many times before. Your son developed diabetes and your friend and neighbor is also a diabetic. You allowed him to die and maybe you even put the candies out of his reach. You knew him better than anyone and you worked out what he'd plotted. You stood, or sat there, and watched him die before your eyes."

"No, Ettie. What you said the first time was right."

Kelly folded his arms across his chest. "Would you be prepared to take a lie detector test?"

"No. Why should I?"

"To prove your innocence, Mother."

"Be quiet, Simon. You always were a stupid boy."

Kelly frowned. "Mrs. Graber, you had the motive and you were there at the same time he died."

"Albie was left the money, not me."

"Mamm!" Albie stared at his mother with hurt written all over his face. "Were you there when he drew his last breath, *Mamm?"*

"Yes, I was. He killed himself, I didn't do anything. He was a horrible man and even though he promised me the world, I knew he'd never change. I didn't do anything wrong." She turned around, looked at the detective and lifted her chin. "I didn't kill him. I had nothing to do with it."

Detective Kelly stared at her. "That's where you're wrong. By doing nothing, you did something." He pressed a couple of buttons on his phone and two uniformed officers appeared at the door.

"I was pleased he died after everything he put me through. He used to give the boys a thrashing with the strap for nothing at all. If they weren't sitting straight enough at the dinner table, or for speaking to him the wrong way. It was like walking on eggshells every single day."

"It was a long time ago, *Mamm.*"

"I remember it as if it was yesterday."

"Why did you take his money?" Simon asked.

"I deserved something for all the dark years I'd spent with him. Anyway, he gave me the money."

Tyson put his arm around Sophie. "We should go."

Sophie looked back at the detective. "I admit I watched him die and didn't do anything to stop it. But, I didn't kill him. Am I free to go?"

"For now. I'll be in touch."

"How could you do that, Mother? How could you watch him die?" Simon asked.

"He killed the person I used to be. Don't you get it? He killed me. It was justification."

Sophie and Tyson hurried out the door, past the officers who were standing just inside. Ettie noticed Sophie didn't even look back at her two sons. It was as though she wanted to put them behind her as well, or was she now ashamed of herself for not helping their father?

"We should go, too," Max said to his wife as he rose to his feet. "This has been a dreadful night."

Kelly stepped forward. "I don't think so. There's a slight matter of tampering with evidence, and abuse of a corpse."

"What? She admitted to watching him die and she walks free? I was only covering up for the sake of the family."

Rather than answer Max, Kelly nodded to the officers and they walked over to him. Then he said to Max, "These gentlemen will escort you to the station. You and I need to have a little chat."

Max was ushered out the door while his wife hurried out behind the officers.

Harold stood up and said to Ettie, "Thanks for inviting me and then for making me stay. It was entertaining."

"Oh," Ettie said staring at him as he hurried out the door.

"Does my mother get away with it just like that?" Simon asked the detective.

"That might possibly happen. Unless you know something I don't," Kelly said to Simon.

"She didn't raise a finger. He was a cad, but she might as well have killed him."

"Unless I can prove she tampered with the evidence, or tampered with his body, there's not much I can charge her with. I'm no lawyer, but I believe since you're closely related to the deceased you'll be able to sue her in a civil action for negligent death. The court might find her guilty by her failure to call for help or to administer help herself, and that resulted in his death."

"But she won't end up in jail?"

"If I draw a blank then no, but you can sue her for loss of contributions from the deceased for you, or your children. I've seen it done before. See a lawyer."

"Not much point if she's not going to jail. And what about the money from my father? The verbal deal was she'd pay him back."

"He's not alive to testify to that. There's probably not much that can be done now if there was nothing written down, or no emails or texts."

Simon drew in a couple of sharp breaths.

Kelly said, "Calm down, take a slow breath. This

isn't over yet. With what I've learned tonight I'll go over the evidence once more."

"The system sucks." Simon bounded to his feet and walked out without saying another word.

Everyone else had left, and now there was only Albie. Ettie looked at Albie, feeling deeply sorry for him. He'd had a dreadful life with the beatings, and now he had no comfort from his brother or his mother.

Albie looked up at Ettie. "Is that really how my father died?"

"I'm afraid so."

"He loved her after all. That gives me some small sense of satisfaction."

"It does?" Kelly asked. "The opposite was true for your mother."

"He wasn't an easy person to get along with. The outward Titus Graber was very different for the one I grew up with and the one my mother had to suffer with. We kept quiet about what he was like. Everyone thought he was a good man, and I suppose he was in a way—in his own way." He looked up at Ettie. "How did you figure all this out about my father giving himself a dose of insulin to make himself appear sick?"

"It was something Elsa-May said about liking a challenge and then I caught a glimpse of some recent crosswords he'd done." She recalled the crosswords Kelly had taken into evidence that he briefly allowed her to see. "One of the crosswords was all about love, marriage, and commitment. I knew that crossword was all about Sophie, but then I just had to wait for the pieces to fall together."

He slowly nodded. "Well, thank you for tonight. I know you've done your best to help locate my father's killer. In the end, there was no killer. He was just careless."

"He took a big risk and it didn't pay off," Elsa-May said. "Oh, Ettie, that's what the word was."

"What word?"

"The word I had that Kelly wouldn't allow me to write."

"What was it?"

"Regret."

"Is that it?" Ettie asked. When Elsa-May nodded, Ettie pulled a face. "It's not a very impressive word. I thought it might be a word that meant a large calculated risk or a dangerous risk."

"It makes sense to me," Albie said. "I hope it means he regrets how he raised Simon and me and how he treated my mother."

"*Jah.* I think you're right," Elsa-May said.

Albie smiled and then continued, "My mother used to be kind and sweet and now, as you witnessed tonight, she has a hard streak. *Denke,* Elsa-May, for remembering that word. That word will enable me to move forward."

Elsa-May's face beamed. "You're welcome."

"I need to get down to the station and get a revised statement from Max Burley. Thanks once again for your help, ladies. I'll go through the evidence once more, but I'm certain there won't be any surprises. We'll be able to wrap this thing up now."

"We didn't do much at all," Ettie said.

The detective smiled at them both, said goodbye to Albie, and walked out the door.

"Would you like a cup of hot tea, or perhaps a *kaffe,* Albie?" Ettie asked.

"Nee, denke. All I want to do now is go home." He stood up and the sisters walked him to the door.

Once the horse was clip-clopping down the road, Ettie closed the door and shuffled over to the couch and flung herself on it. Elsa-May opened the dog door for Snowy and, as usual, Snowy ran around sniffing where Detective Kelly had been.

"I'll be glad to go to bed tonight," Ettie said. "It's a sad and sorry thing."

Elsa-May sat in her chair at the same time that Snowy made himself comfortable on his bed in the corner of the room. "Funny how that one word gave Albie comfort."

Ettie closed her heavy eyelids. *"Jah,* it was. It just goes to show how words are powerful things. They can entertain or inform, and apart from that, they can build someone up or tear someone down. Or in his case, it comforted Albie at a low point in his life."

"Hmm," Elsa-May murmured. "Now we know how poor old Titus died, but one thing still puzzles me. What was Sophie looking for when we were hiding in the closet?"

"I'd say she was looking for money and was talking to ... most likely Tyson, her friend, on the cell phone. She knew everyone would've been at the meeting and it was her perfect chance to see what she could take. She was too spooked the day she found Titus nearly dead to look for money. She's not going to admit she owed him anything for the candle store and she's saying it was a gift. From what her son said, I doubt it was a gift at all."

Elsa-May yawned loudly. "Money? She was looking for money, or something of value?"

"I'd say so. It fits like a word in a crossword puzzle."

Elsa-May mumbled something.

"What did you say?" Ettie asked.

When there was no further word from her sister,

Ettie lifted her shoulders off the couch and looked over at Elsa-May to see her eyes closed and her mouth wide open. Then Ettie put her head back down, closed her eyes again and wondered whether Elsa-May had truly remembered that word, or whether she had simply made it up to give Albie some kind of peaceful resolution. It was something her sister would do, and Elsa-May had never been able to remember any of those other words before.

Elsa-May let out the loudest snore Ettie had ever heard, causing Snowy to leap to his feet. All Ettie could do was cover her mouth and giggle.

Thank you for reading The Last Word.

THE NEXT BOOK IN THE SERIES

Book 15
Old Promises

Unyielding in her conviction that her daughter Myra couldn't so much as squish a bug, Ettie Smith's world is sent spinning when Myra is ensnared in a murder accusation.

Teamed up with her sister, Ettie embarks on the monumental task of absolving her daughter's name, uprooting secrets that were intended to stay buried with the dust bunnies of history. As they delicately reconstruct the jigsaw of the victim's final day, unexpected truths bubble to the surface.

Could it be that Myra is hiding a past that's been quietly ticking away in the corners of her world?

THE NEXT BOOK IN THE SERIES

Buckle up for a wild ride - this whimsical mystery will have you darting between twists, gasping at revelations, and thoroughly entranced until the last word.

ABOUT SAMANTHA PRICE

Samantha Price is a USA Today bestselling and Kindle All Stars author of Amish romance books and cozy mysteries. She was raised Brethren and has a deep affinity for the Amish way of life, which she has explored extensively with over a decade of research.

She is mother to two pampered rescue cats, and a very spoiled staffy with separation issues.

www.SamanthaPriceAuthor.com

ETTIE SMITH AMISH MYSTERIES

Book 1 Secrets Come Home
Book 2 Amish Murder
Book 3 Murder in the Amish Bakery
Book 4 Amish Murder Too Close
Book 5 Amish Quilt Shop Mystery
Book 6 Amish Baby Mystery
Book 7 Betrayed
Book 8 Amish False Witness
Book 9 Amish Barn Murders
Book 10 Amish Christmas Mystery
Book 11 The Amish Cat Caper
Book 12 Lost
Book 13 Amish Cover-Up
Book 14 The Last Word
Book 15 Old Promises
Book 16 Amish Mystery at Rose Cottage

Book 17 Plain Secrets
Book 18 Fear Thy Neighbor
Book 19 Amish Winter Murder Mystery
Book 20 Amish Scarecrow Murders
Book 21 Threadly Secret
Book 22 Sugar and Spite
Book 23 A Puzzling Amish Murder
Book 24 Amish Dead and Breakfast
Book 25 Amish Mishaps and Murder
Book 26 A Deadly Amish Betrayal
Book 27 Amish Buggy Murder

ALL SAMANTHA PRICE BOOK SERIES

Amish Maids Trilogy

Amish Love Blooms

Amish Misfits

The Amish Bonnet Sisters

Amish Women of Pleasant Valley

Ettie Smith Amish Mysteries

Amish Secret Widows' Society

Expectant Amish Widows

ALL SAMANTHA PRICE BOOK SERIES

Seven Amish Bachelors

Amish Foster Girls

Amish Brides

Amish Romance Secrets

Amish Christmas Books

Amish Wedding Season

Printed in Great Britain
by Amazon